OUTSIDERS

An Anthology

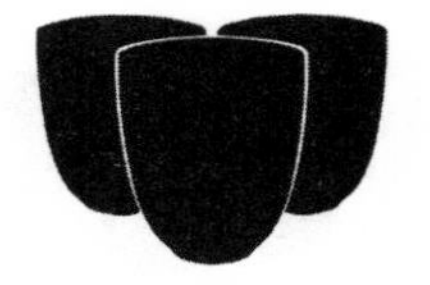

Published in 2020 by

3 of Cups Press

London

References to websites were correct at the time of writing.

Paperback ISBN 9781916263901

eBook ISBN 9781916263918

Printed and bound by CPI Group (UK) Ltd,

Croydon, CR0 4YY

Cover design by Rebecca Strickson

www.3ofcups.co.uk

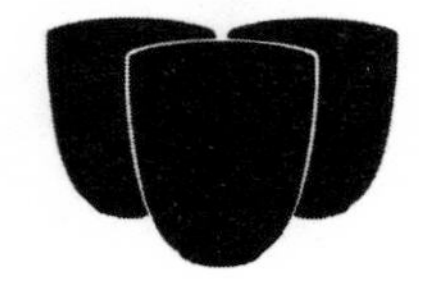

Contents

FOREWORD

Irenosen Okojie

> The outsider will say, in fact, as a woman,
> I have no country. As a woman I want no country.
> As a woman my country is the whole world.
>
> *Virginia Woolf*

The notion of outsider women has long existed within modern consciousness. From ancient times to our current era, the renegade, the outlander, the fringe dweller has always operated, thrived and survived, both in life and the writer's imagination. How we understand them remains endlessly fascinating, even paradoxical at times. Do social circumstances play a part or do individuals come into the world with that feeling of fragmentation, isolation and the inner loneliness of being removed from what is presented as the norm? When I reflect on women who epitomise the outsider, I think of Zora Neale Hurston, Mary Shelley, Ursula K. Le Guin and Audre Lorde. These writers blazed trails when it seemed there was no space for them in hostile landscapes. They found ways to make their voices heard, show us new perspectives. At its crux, the outsider is one who does not belong. These writers turned ideas of exclusion on its head along with shunning societal expectations of what women writers can and should write about. They created stories and worlds which transcend time, enriching us, encouraging women to rediscover works that act as torches when the world appears to be going backwards.

There is no getting away from the fact that it has been a terrible few years. The rise of the Me Too movement saw shocking stories on the systemic abuse of women flood the zeitgeist. Brexit Britain has exhausted a lot of us, Trumpian shenanigans leave people in varying states of shock and weekly disbelief, news cycles providing glimpses beyond our bubbles possess a dystopian inevitability. The world is at a tipping point. In this charged, political climate, never has the term 'outsider' been more pertinent. Never has the cost or value of what that means seemed more complicated to quantify. Never has there been such a necessity to take a peek between the crevices. Never have we needed women's voices more.

For women writers like me who are othered on several levels, existence as an outsider is a normal state of being. We find the beauty and power in it. We gravitate towards people like us. We create communities, friendships, spaces that deepen our understandings of each other. We bring our forms of magic and chaos to the fore. A writer's gift is to make the outsider the centre, rendering what is deemed invisible real and indelible. We are makers who mine for stories beyond labels, using our agency as creators to realise the lofty ambitions of producing tales that give readers fresh insights.

We must always reach for new deconstructions so we do not fall prey to narrow mindedness, suspicion and lack of empathy. The wonder of stories is that they add dimensions to our understanding of the human condition. In this seminal anthology, the offerings of what difference means from these magnificent women writers are not teachable moments but explorations of the gulfs in between ways of being. They are transformative acts. A story can change lives or become an evolving blueprint one returns to. These stories in varied settings traversing genre, subject matter and form invoke other versions of us, snapshots of multiple possibilities, glimpses of what past and future lives look like. Here, the mythic and modern interpretations coalesce, framing how a sense of belonging or lack thereof shapes us. Each woman's voice gives us radical new insights. Each story is a world to enter, prophetically and intelligently imagining the unseen, different selves. The range and quality of stories illustrates the power of literature to challenge reader's perspectives as well as the artist's agency to respond to the complexities of our time with verve and intelligence.

To be an outsider is to be unmoored where definitions via race, ethnicity, gender, class, sexuality or the intersection of the aforementioned set individuals apart. Often, an outsider is shunned, sneered at, reviled or reduced to invisibilities away from the norm. But living as an outsider comes with a sense of liberation, being unshackled from societal expectations and the freedom to define one's cultural values. This celebration of outsiders gives permission to revel in the power of stories to impact us on cellular levels. These triumphant, visceral pieces expand our ideas of what it means to exist on the fringes in some form or another. Reading the stories in this collection encourages us to strengthen our capacity to identify with others in all their glorious differences, to take the empathetic step to explore the mysteries of what sets us apart is to know the human condition a little better, and to see our worlds open up even more.

INTRODUCTION

Alice Slater

Keiko Furukura. Eileen Dunlop. Merricat Blackwood. I love outsiders. I love bold voices, and I love characters that go against the grain. Don't we all?

Narratives about outsiders are captivating, because the reader is always an outsider to the world within the pages of a book. We relate to the ingenue narrator of *Rebecca* because we're all strangers to Manderley. We're all freshman at Hampden College, where Richard pines for the mysterious Ancient Greek clique from afar. We're all watching the Lisbon girls from a distance. We're all stoating around New York calling everyone phonies.

But as much as the reader will always relate to outsiders, narratives about outsiders that are intrinsically different to us promote empathy and understanding, and serve as a record for how things can be for those on the fringes, living in the margins, ostracized, left behind.

In this anthology, you're going to meet both Merricats and Holdens. You're going to meet outsiders who are monstrous; outsiders who are unwelcome; outsiders who are teenagers; outsiders who are lovers; outsiders who are queer; outsiders who are othered because of where they were born, where they grew up, where they emigrated to; you're going to meet loners, biters, and people who are uncomfortable in their own skin – literally. You're going to meet communities of outsiders who are dangerous, and communities that are dangerous to outsiders.

We all secretly see ourselves as outsiders in one way or another. We're all the protagonists of our own private narratives, and we experience the world from a perspective shaped by our wants and needs, our politics and our regrets, our memories and the things we choose to forget.

But to be an outsider means there must be an inside too – a community, a majority, a mainstream, an in-crowd. We all have that duality within us: no man is an island, and we're all part of something larger than ourselves. There's strength in numbers. It's human nature to form communities, but it's our social responsibility to recognise who our communities might be overlooking, and to ensure no one is left behind.

2020

CONTENT NOTES

WENDIGO

Julia Armfield

Stop me
if you've heard this one before: the lands up north,
Hoar-bent, frost-locked, need deeper plows
To dig them. Here is one.
Beowulf – Meaghan Purvis

Have you ever heard the one, he says, *about the girl in the car and the fingers scratching.* He mimes claws, reaches down to scrabble her hair, but she's already doing the same to him, pulling at his knitted hat until he slaps her. *And the fingers on the roof,* she says, *and it's the dead boyfriend and the guy's strung him up above the car. Yeah. I've heard that one before.*

He is leaning up against the sea wall because his side hurts and the sky is weeping its colours – long drain of white across the surface of the sea. His voice is like chalk, the gentle drag of it, and she thinks about cliffs and then about blackboards, about sidewalk games and murder victims marked out in silhouette, about pool cues and pigment dust and Pica. This happens a lot, this categorisation. Someone says *aluminium* and she makes a list: *Coca-Cola, tinfoil, patio chair.* Standing next to him but a little way removed, she thinks about the way they used to learn things; one holding up an item that the other had provided and naming it loudly: *oven glove, umbrella, clock, Cup-a-Soup.*

The wind is high – a pummelling thing that seems to lift and push at the ocean like fingers clawed in bedclothes. They are just beyond the beach, on the concrete flat that slopes towards the headland, and she wishes she had worn something thicker than a denim jacket.

I think, he said in the car a little earlier, *I think I can make it that far.* They had been driving since daybreak and she had mostly been telling stories to keep him awake. *Remember the one about the petrol station, about the man in the back seat holding the axe.* They have always done this, played at monsters, swapped stories that pretend a reality their ubiquity belies. Everyone knows the one about the man in the back seat holding the axe because it happened to everyone's second cousin. A folk tale, in as much as a folk tale also means a lie.

She hoped they might be able to go down onto the sand, but by the time they arrived it was touch-and-go as to whether she'd be able to get him out of the car. *Don't touch me*, he said, and then, *help me up.* When he leaned against her, she thought of flying buttresses. Thought, in quick succession: *masonry, gothic architecture, catacombs*.

He has always been taller than her; a dark shape, stretching up towards the sky like some terrible fault in the landscape – a split within whatever view he inhabits. She is smaller, though still tall, the hunching gait of something difficult. They do not fit easily inside the car. When they spend their nights in motels, their feet stick out over the end of the beds.

Do you think, he is saying now, *that if I die here, you'll be able to bury me.* She looks out over the sand and imagines how much of it would have to be displaced to make space for him. *I think I'd rather you didn't,* she says and then shrugs.

* * *

They came south several years ago, winding down from where they were before: nuclear country, soft polluted soil. They were younger then, possibly taller. Over time, her hunch has become more conspicuous, his legs taking on the aspect of something crushed – a spider caught beneath the rim of a glass. They were loping creatures once, the long strides of giants moving over sleeping cities. He moves slowly now, cautious as something on a wire. Their heads cramp automatically sideways when they slide into the car.

In the old days, they travelled fast, eating up country, repeating words to one another until they'd learned them the whole way through: *viaduct, Viagra, Ovaltine.* Their vocabulary came in part from the car radio, which they played constantly, and their patterns of speech were littered at first with words almost entirely peculiar to music of the 70s and 80s (*groovy, fever*) until it occurred to them to move from an easy listening channel to all-talk. They drove by day and in the early morning, stopping on the outskirts of towns when the night came on and proceeding further on foot.

In the old days, it was easier. They moved soundlessly, no one saw them arrive.

* * *

Well what about this one, he says to her, elbows back against the sea wall, needle of pain in the left thread of his eye, *there's a woman you conjure to foretell the future. Bloody Mary. You say her name into a mirror three times and she appears, but summoning her isn't always safe.* She is unsure what to say to this as, again, it is a story she has heard before, so she simply inspects her hands, the mottled skin between the knuckles, and wonders what she's going to do with him when this is over.

Beneath his coat, the fabric of his sweatshirt is blackening, dark stain like an absence, like a hole punched through a wall. It is Tuesday, curtained windows on the scant collection of beach-adjacent houses she had noticed on the drive down. She imagines going back to one of these houses, ducking down to meet the eyes of whoever answers her knock and telling them *please, I don't know what to do.*

Why don't we try to walk, she says instead, looking down towards the sand again – ridge-cut by headland winds, a queasy ripple running perpendicular to the tide. They came from ground like this, wind-ravaged, though different in its mineral content, the ratio of rock to clay. Where they came from, a thin reed of something poisonous bled through the topsoil, a dark infecting trace stretching down towards the place where things grew.

* * *

Once, they had come to a town in its first insanity of Christmas lighting, red neon holly wreaths and reindeer suspended in flight across the bow of the shopping precinct. They moved through the streets that night without speaking – 3am, witching hour in full illumination – but when they found what they were looking for, she still set her fingers to her lips.

Afterwards, they were performing the necessary rituals (she keeps wet wipes in her rucksack, a value pack of chewing gum) when he huffed a sudden laugh, bent down to peel a flier from the ground. They were somewhere between streets, narrow lane leading off from the highroad, overshadowed by buildings on either side, and his voice echoed thinly as he read: *Legendary radio DJ Les Brown from popular morning show Get Up With Les switches on this year's town centre Christmas lights.* She looked at him, the endless line of him, perhaps as tall as the buildings that boxed them in. She thought to herself: *building, window, invasion*, had pictured the curl of his fingers around the outer edge of a windowsill. She wiped her teeth with an index finger – copper taste, the zing of licked batteries. *Legendary*, he repeated, over and over, holding the flier aloft, and she played along: *Legendary, mythical, fabled, monstrous, foul.*

* * *

She leads him down the sand, one hand at his elbow, catching his side when he stumbles. It is still early enough for them to be the only people on the beach, though she had half-expected a dog-walker, an early surfer – salt smack of someone unfamiliar, wool-swaddle, hair and skin. When this happens, the far-off waft of someone, she has learned to clamp her tongue against her teeth to prevent the flooding of saliva; drip-choke of sudden hunger pooling backwards down her throat.

I feel bad, he says, *this isn't helping.* The throb of his side seems to travel into hers by sheer proximity. She dips her chin into her chest to guard against the wind.

* * *

At first (at very first) they had been content to roam, moving the way their bodies allowed them – the writhe, the shiver, the slink.

How they first emerged was never clear to them, they simply *were* one day – same as anything – broken earth and the cake of soil crusted up into the corners of their mouths. They learned, in stages, to move their jaws and lips and finally to talk. His voice, the first time he used it, was like clay, mined from earth, the sound of something packed tight and gradually excavated. He spoke first, made a noise that wasn't a word but which she would later misremember as *hunger.* It was the first noise to draw her attention; to drag her wet and invertebrate through the soil towards him. Above them that first night hung impossible stars and the wheel of the sky like something balanced on a tilting table, ready to slip. They knitted themselves together in pieces, became bodies that shuddered and sat.

Over time, they learned to walk, to move in ways that brought them closer to the ordinary. They stood up, looked about themselves and realised they would have to travel if they wanted to survive. *Hunger,* she still thinks, often just before sleeping. *Hunger, starvation, craving, yearning, longing, appetite, want.*

* * *

They come to a halt some yards before the water's edge when he decides with no forewarning that he cannot stand. She releases him without making a decision to do so, watches him go down with a detachment that seems appropriate to the fall of something vast, too big to care about on any personal level. The Roman Empire, the sinking of the Titanic. Tragedies, in their most generic sense, but not in a way that means anything to her. She only feels it briefly, this curious apathy, the sense that what is happening is just another story that she might hear and disregard: *Did you ever hear the one about the sinking ship, the crumbling citadel, did you hear about the figure on the beach, the way his legs went out from under him.* Coming to herself after a moment, she staggers down to her knees beside him, clutches at his elbows and then at his neck. She tries to recall how she has fixed things in the past, tries to picture the contents of her rucksack: loose change and antiseptic wipes, six packs of spearmint gum, three gold teeth she had found she couldn't swallow, a clump of hair, a box of Elastoplast.

Come on now, she says, tries to recollect the plots of the radio soaps from which she first learned to speak in full sentences, *come on now, you're ok, you're going to make it.* In their early driving days, after they switched from the music stations, she had become briefly obsessed with radio serials – the low-stakes dramas and amateurish sound effects, the sudden stops and cliffhanger endings. Her voice now is an imitation of that. She is thinking of an episode of a day-time drama she once listened to; a woman's voice soothing a man through partial impalement by a piece of farming machinery. *You're going to make it,* she says again, *just stay awake. Come on now, come on now, you're okay.* Amateur dramatics, all this, lines learned to move the action forward. She remembers bits and pieces of the dialogue but she can't remember whether the man in the radio drama lived or died.

* * *

They had eaten to keep going, followed their appetites across country, away from the first polluted place. Pain in the bones when they failed to sate their hunger, pain in the eyes and up the backs of the legs. Once they started to drive, they tuned the radio only very occasionally to local news channels, learning words like *ravening,* like *marauding,* like *attack*.

One night, they came upon a town that lay asleep behind closed shutters, striding inwards from the curve of a road that fell beneath a protective line of trees. He whistled as they walked – a toothsome sound, something new he had learned to do with his mouth – and the noise echoed back to them in the valley-dip that held the town like something offered on a palm. She smelled it before she saw it: hot blood, the way it slugs through sleeping bodies. *D'you know the one,* he said, *about the monster who visited the hall every night to feast on men until the hero did away with him, and the second monster who went on after him, who came to wreak havoc in revenge.* They had been listening to a drama on the radio that afternoon, an ancient story filled with mists and murky waters and names she couldn't imagine how to spell. *Of course I know that one*, she said, *we just heard it.* He quirked his eyebrow at her, set his sights towards the town.

(Ways to eat: perhaps three in total. In pieces, insufficiently or all at once. When they approached a town, they did so always in hopes of a feast and in expectation of setbacks. It was too difficult, increasingly so, to proceed unchecked, to grab at something and carry it off without finding themselves pursued.)

* * *

In the sand, his shape is that of something scored, as though his coffin-lines are cut around him. Even now, she can't be entirely sure what is wrong. The dark in his side is growing wider, as though something in his internal make-up has soured and caved in. She wonders briefly about starvation, tries to remember the last time they managed to eat without interruption, but if that were the issue then presumably she would be fading too. Something simpler than that, she supposes. They come from bad soil, are perhaps made up of it. Unstable bodies, grown from septic earth.

I don't feel good, he says, and she feels this the way she has always felt it: when he eats and her throat fills with air as if in mimicry, when he hurts and her body sings with an answering ache. They come from the same soil, rose up together one day like plane trees, and she worries this means that his sickness must also be hers. *We're not the same*, she wants to say, *I'm the second monster, not the first. I'm supposed to go on after him.*

* * *

She had watched, once, on the outskirts of a town before it slept. The lights of a pub and its hanging sign, the shuffle and hiss of a bus stopping to disgorge its contents. Mist-slick cobbles, parked cars and upstairs windows open half an inch.

She watched a gaggle of women rounding a corner, four of them walking in tandem, black tights and sudden gnashing talk: *I heard he lives with his mother, I heard he has ringworm, I heard that after he sleeps with a woman he cries.* They collected beneath a lamppost, bright-haired, shrieking and sharing cigarettes. One holding a box of fried chicken, another an asthma inhaler which she jammed in her mouth and depressed with a noisy zip. *Did you hear what happened with Sarah's boyfriend, did you hear about Gary, did you hear the thing he said.*

From the safety of the shadows, she watched them, pushed her face into silent imitation of their expressions: eyebrows up, chin down, mouth wide and whaling. *Give me a drag of that,* one said to another, reaching for a cigarette. *Feels like rain*, said one, *this chicken tastes like fish,* and she mouthed along. Later, she would pick them off, stalk one and then another, push her fingers into flesh pickled sour with alcohol like something plucked from a jar, open her mouth. For now, however, she only watched, staving off her hunger with the duelling need for something else, something other, the words she mouthed in tandem with the women on the corner: *It's cold. Let's go inside. I'm knackered. One more cigarette.*

We aren't like them, he had always said, leading her through empty streets on the hunt for what they wanted. *If nothing else, we're bigger.* She nodded and said nothing, mimicking the faces of the people they saw when she knew he wasn't looking.

* * *

He has been dying since before she started the car this morning, holding his body like something he might spill from a bowl. Perhaps it was always inevitable. She sits beside him, seep of wet sand through her jeans, and listens to his breathing.

Lying down in the sand like an animal with its belly exposed, he inhales, exhales. Seems to pause as if unsure between the one and the other. She has seen people die, of course, has chewed untold amounts of gum and flossed her teeth to free herself from their specific flavour. Dying people rattle and so now does he, which seems odd. He isn't 'people', after all, and nor is she. Something other, they have always been: hungry ghosts, one shape and then another looming up towards the sky.

She remembers listening to the radio - the story about two monsters, Grendel and his mother: half-murdered creature staggering down towards the water, another striding out to take his place. A myth or a fairy tale, she isn't sure of the appropriate label: *fantasy, fable, allegory, imaginary, unreal*. When the first monster died, the second monster entered the narrative, but only for as long as she lived, which wasn't long at all.

Do you think, he had said once, long ago – fiddling with the buttons on the car radio, moving past sports and weather, pop classics and local news – *do you think we'll eat it all, eventually. The towns, the cities, all of it*. He was vast, snapping his fingers to a snatch of music, confident in their ability to continue unimpeded for as long as they needed to eat. *Hey, here's one for you – a girl's babysitting in a house and she starts to get phone calls – I'm sure I haven't told you this one before.*

She looks at him now, the spill of his body, the way he seems to take up as many miles as there is coastline. He will die soon, she knows, and she will register nothing but hunger, press her fingers into his flesh and act the only way either of them have ever known how. Unhook her jaw, thick spool of white saliva. Floss afterwards, chew her spearmint gum. *Have you ever heard the one*, they will say, *about the monster who died and the monster who outlived him. Did you hear what she did, where she went afterwards. Do you know where she is right now.*

There is a town barely half a mile from shore – she glimpsed its rooftops from the car on the drive down, the curtained windows and the walls. Later on, she will brush her knees, wipe her mouth, pull her jacket tight around her and stand, preparatory to wending her way back in. When she leaves, the tide will wash away the imprint of his body, sea urchins like so many eyes unpeeled across the rocks.

Did you ever hear the one about the monster. Do you hear her coming now.

FRANCINE

Anna Wood

Turn right at the helter skelter and keep going till you see the standpipe with the red bucket. We're just there, with the French flag flying (none of us is French).

A year ago we were in the same spot and the sky was just as clear and sunny, although it was much hotter. We arrived in the middle of the Tuesday afternoon. Jenny was driving the purple Renault with Luigi, Kate and Al, and then there was Mandy and Stella and me in my car. There were a few tents and tipis up in the Park Stage camping field but we had room and time to walk around, tutting at the guy ropes, considering the slopes, the lumps and prickly bits, where the toilets were, where people might piss against the fence or the trees, where the standpipe was, what route we'd take back in the pitch black with booze-heavy feet and fuzzy heads.

And then we decided on a spot and dropped our bags and tents to claim our territory. We dragged a couple of hay bales over from a pile by the wristband checkpoint – these would be seats around our little campfire. 'Is it okay to take these?' said Mandy, and I said 'Oh, I think so,' because we weren't exactly sneaking off with them and we could put them back if they were needed. 'They're to soak up mud on the paths if it rains, aren't they? And it's not going to rain.' The ground was dry and the sun was hot.

Stella and Mandy were mixing St-Germain and vodka with some lemonade. Mandy had brought strawberries and elderberries and these were also going into the giant plastic jug she had. No ice. The jug had 'MALIBU' written across it. She had snaffled it from a photoshoot at work earlier in the summer, the coconut booze long gone. She was wearing a ground-length dress, flowery, and her dark hair was down loose over her shoulders with flowers and grass stuck in it. Mandy was always the softest and sweetest, the one who provided cake on birthdays, and who felt sympathy for even the most obnoxious people, but who also fought – with bared teeth and thrown-back shoulders – when her friends were under attack, and dismissed those who weren't good enough ('Fucking loser mummy's-boy prick,' she might say, while giving you a warm, forever cuddle).

Stella's depths were just as deep, but better hidden. And she was just as good at late nights and dancing and excited wide-eyed conversations. I'd met her years ago – Mandy brought her to Del's house party in Southwark and she passed out in the front room ('She's gone non-verbal but she's breathing,' Mandy had told me, stroking Stella's hair). That memory of a snuggly, helpless drug baby had since been replaced by this Stella, with her legs and her cheekbones and her fuck-it-let's-do-it enthusiasms. She was fishing the boozy fruit out of the jug and eating it, wearing a bright yellow vest and denim shorts, cut off so you could see the pockets poking out the bottom. She had flowers in her hair as well, because Mandy had put them there, a cluster of blossoms from the tree a few yards away.

I was putting my tent up. I had a mallet and an airbed with an electric pump and I was happy. Mandy and Stella were sharing a four-man tent, and it was spread on the ground ready to put up, after they'd downed some of the cocktail but before it got dark. They had a second, smaller tent for stuff – clothes, boots, bottles – so that the main tent could be their boudoir, their sleeping quarters. Our group was seven tents all together, a happy hippy heptagon. The others had put up their tents in minutes, headed straight out of our field to explore. Jenny wanted a henna tattoo. Luigi and Kate wanted food. I don't know what Al wanted, but he was with Luigi and Kate, carrying an open bottle of Merlot and a rollie or a spliff, wearing orange short-shorts (no top, hard brown body) and singing *Hot Fun in the Summertime*. He walked a few feet behind them, doing little sideways skips and sways, singing the backing vocals as well as the lead, occasionally dancing up to Luigi or Kate so he could sing 'High high high hiiiiigh' in their ear.

When I was all done I sat on a bale and drank from the jug. Mandy and Stella were standing on each side of their big tent, looking at it. The grass was long in our field but would get squashed in the next day or so. The helter skelter (actually just a rickety tower covered in rainbow-coloured streamers) had a few people at the top, looking out over the site. From there they could see all the acres, the stages and campsites and food stalls and dance tents and toilets and room for a quarter of a million people, a town without buildings, dozens of canvas villages all stuck together, just for a few days. A Brigadoon. They probably couldn't hear much from up there though. I heard the music from the hospitality tent near our camp, but I didn't recognise it. Something proggy and pompous. I heard the food stall across the fence playing *Club Tropicana*, and the two men working there both whistling along. I loved it all. The smell of frying meat and doughnuts mixed with the smell of warm earth and blossoms.

This was all before we'd ever seen or heard anything of Francine. The three of us finished the Malibooze, Mandy mixed another jugful and we took it with us, went to lounge about in the Healing Fields. A naked couple, a man and a woman all leathery and smiling, were walking around hand-in-hand, chatting and looking at the stalls and the tipis. We were working to shake off our London snarkiness – we exchanged glances when we saw the couple, but our faces were fond, like 'Ah, bless the old hippies'. And I was a bit jealous. I wondered what it would be like to walk about with your here-we-are tits out and your here-I-am belly fed by the sunshine, to just think, 'Well, isn't this a beautiful body, all mine and warm and part of the grand scheme of things?'

Jenny found us there and for an hour or two we lay on the grass, admired her new henna tattoo (she had a big sunshine around her belly button). We talked about the six days and nights ahead, sleeping in tents, cold when we went to sleep and baking hot when we woke up, dehydrated and half-cooked and doing a shame-and-highlights inventory of the night before. As it got dusky in the pinking sky, we headed back to basecamp. Luigi had started a fire and Kate was sitting with someone, someone I assumed she knew. A young, smooth-skinned woman, with two dark blonde plaits hanging down her back, wearing denim dungarees. She and Kate were on one of the bales, smoking a spliff. 'This is Francine,' Kate told us, and passed the spliff along. They went back to their silence. I noticed we had eight tents now.

'You hungry?' I asked Kate, and looked at Francine. Her head was tipped back so her chin pointed to me. She gave me a huge grin, startling really. Her whole face seemed to widen and I felt a bit giddy.

'I got tacos,' Kate said. 'You want some?' She passed me a cardboard tray of clumped-up cheesy salsa and chips, still warm, and good and salty. I sat on the next bale, watched the fire as Luigi tried to prod some life into it, chomped on the tacos. Kate went to get more wood from the patch of trees further up the hill and Luigi was singing along to something on his tinny little iPod dock. He was doing little bum-shakes, his shoulders shrugged up and down in a groovy-dad dance. Mandy passed me a newly full Malibu jug and I poured a cup for me and one for Stella. She handed it straight to Francine and turned back to me for more. Francine gave us another grin, only slightly less powerful than the last.

I intercepted Kate on her way back, helped her with the crunchy spindly branches, and asked, 'Who's that?'

'Dunno. She seems alright though. I think she might be a mate of Al's.'

Later when I asked Al about Francine, he suggested she might be a mate of Kate's, then pointed out what a beautiful smile she had.

There were no bands on that night, not officially, but lots of parties and live music all over the place. The seven of us headed out to see a Hawkwind splinter group that was playing in the Dead Zone at dusk. Kate asked Francine if she would like to come with us, with a high-pitched voice and raised eyebrows, as if she was asking a puppy to come walkies, or a child if they needed a pee. The rest of us were already heading off.

'I'm fine,' said Francine, still sitting on her bale, so Kate smiled and turned round and caught up with the rest of us.

We split into two groups but then we all found each other again, at the front, where it wasn't packed and where we could see the crusty foamy mouth of the man booming into the microphone. 'I'm charged with cosmic energy,' he sang, had been singing for 40 years and still meant it, I reckon. There was a saxophone making space noises, and weirdly lazy drumming, and a superfast, belting guitarist, and keyboards that didn't seem to be doing anything. The crowd was mostly grey-haired double-denim men, singing along, sometimes shouting the lyrics or thrusting their beer in the air, oblivious to us or else quite happy to have us jostling into their gig. I did a few loops around the podium which stood a couple of feet high in the middle of the small crowd. I wanted to walk through clumps of people I didn't know, look at faces and smile. Stella and Mandy stayed at the stage with the others, faces shining, shoulders rocking left-then-right, entertained, occasionally entranced, maybe a little disconcerted by the old man screeching and booming at them. It was more crowded now and I slipped through sideways back to Mandy's side.

Later that night we jitterbugged with pretty teenage boys at an all-night diner. When we got back, Francine was still sitting on the hay bale. It was as if she hadn't moved. The fire was still giving out heat, and she was humming to herself. I don't think we said a word to her, we just faded into our tents.

On the Wednesday night we found a packed, dark techno room that you could only get to by crawling for several yards on your hands and knees through a metal-and-canvas tunnel. On the Thursday we sat round a fire with two Scottish boys we met in the Healing Fields and took it in turns to play songs on ipods plugged into Luigi's stereo – three songs at a time 'and no shit ones,' as Mandy explained, 'or you miss a turn and you have to go and get more cider.'

We established little daytime routines across the festival. We bought breakfast at the caravan where you could get hot porridge with brown sugar, and found a shortcut across a tiny stream through to the area with fairylit trees in plant pots where cute artist boys were doing voodoo face painting and spooky storytelling. We walked to the edges of the site, just to have a look at the huge fence which had foundations too so you couldn't dig under it. There was a spot a few minutes from our camping area, by the taco stall and the gin tent, which became our place for meeting up – 'I'm going for a wander, I'll see you back at The Place.' There was always a very high chance that someone you knew was about to amble past that spot.

Francine didn't go anywhere, as far as I could tell. I hadn't seen her eat, or drink, or even go to the toilets. On the Thursday afternoon Luigi gave her his jacket because it was getting cold. We were all goosepimply sitting near the fire and Francine was there in her dungarees and her soft bare arms. Kate asked if she was warm enough and Francine said she was fine, but Luigi still picked his coat up out of the front of their tent and draped it over her shoulders. A couple of hours later I saw her away from the tents for the first time, when a few of us were heading to the main stage – it had warmed up again and she was lying on Luigi's coat, eyes closed to the sunshine, arms spread above her head. I watched her for a few seconds and then kept walking, didn't mention it to anyone. That night as we were heading out she wasn't back at basecamp yet but when we came back there was a torch glow from inside her little tent so we knew she was home safe.

'Is she real?' said Stella, on the Friday afternoon. We were eating tacos and watching The Abyssinians at the Jazz World Stage.

'I don't know,' I said. And I didn't. We hadn't really discussed Francine and we'd barely spoken to her. Every morning when I woke up she was already up and dressed and sitting on a hay bale. I would say 'Morning' and she would nod, maybe smile, and then I'd get on with the day, we all would, bustling and chatting or lurching with hangovers around this calm, still woman with the plaits and the smile.

'She doesn't say much does she?' Mandy said, with no trace of irritation. But I found it irritating. I had brought her a coffee and a flapjack that morning and she had taken them without saying thank you.

'I don't know what she's been eating,' I said. 'That's why I got her breakfast this morning. She doesn't seem to eat or piss or wash or anything.'

'She's eating clouds and drinking air,' said Stella, who wasn't even stoned.

'She hasn't seen a single band either,' said Mandy. 'What is she doing here? Why is she camping with us?'

'What IS going on?' said Stella, and she was laughing, all three of us laughed. Francine had a sweet smile, and she wasn't doing any harm, and she was outnumbered.

When we got back to base, Francine was in her tent and the boys had the stereo on. They'd been talking about it, too. Al whispered, 'We thought we could wait until she's asleep and then move all our tents to the next field.'

'Just unpeg them and lift them right up. Really quietly,' Luigi was saying.

'We're going in a couple of days anyway,' Mandy said. They were joking, though, and then Francine came out of her tent.

'Hey Francine,' I smiled, and held my bottle of vodka out to her. 'You want to come over to the Park Stage with us? We're getting magic tofu curry on the way there.'

'Do you have any money?' said Mandy, and we all went quiet, a bit embarrassed by the bluntness and listening for the answer.

'I'm fine,' said Francine, and she took the vodka from me, sat down on the hay bale where Luigi had shuffled up to make room.

'Are you meeting friends here or anything?' said Stella. It was like we'd broken the embarrassment ice and she just jumped right in. 'This weekend, I mean. Are your friends camping in this field?'

Luigi looked like he was going to be sick. Jenny and Kate stared at the ground like little kids being told off at school.

'Everyone's a friend at Glastonbury,' said Al. We mumbled agreements, relaxed our shoulders a little. Francine sat watching us as if she was watching television.

'Come to the Park Stage with us,' I said. I wanted to see her walk, talk, step outside of our circle of tents again.

'I didn't mean to be rude,' said Mandy. 'I can lend you money if you need some. Or I'll just give you a tenner, it doesn't matter.'

'That's okay, I'm fine,' said Francine, and smiled another blaster at Mandy. She took a sip, a decent-sized sip though, from the vodka and looked at the dwindling fire. She did look happy on that hay bale.

'Why are you camping here, Francine?' I said, and felt like a bully. I thought perhaps we were all bullies. Francine was fine, though. She just sat on the hay bale, smiled at me and drank some more of my vodka. Al gave her his half-smoked spliff and then we went to the Park Stage, left her there sitting on her own.

'I didn't mean to be rude,' said Mandy again, many hours later.

We were near the top of a hill and it was full daylight, the murmuring excitement of dawn long gone. We were dabbing our fingers into various little plastic bags, sipping cherry schnapps from Jenny's hipflask to take the taste away. I watched the skin on the backs of my hands shrinking and crinkling. There were clusters and circles and pairs of people covering the hillside, but we were a few metres from the closest group. It was just me and Mandy and Stella and Jenny. The earth beneath me felt not much different to the sky above me, as if they were as solid as each other. When I leaned back I felt myself fizzing into the earth. Stella leaned back too, rested her head on my hip, and our eyes soaked up the sky.

That night we had danced in one of the smaller tents, solid smiling dancing for three or four hours. Something like a happy boredom would begin to sink into my bones, an active relaxation, almost an anxiety because it felt so good and things couldn't stay that way. Then I'd notice a cute boy or a different song would start and I'd be away again, dancing, smiling, sometimes just spinning round. And things were just as good when we were sitting on that hillside, watching people dance to no music, and talk and laugh and kiss. Gifts and pleasures disappear around corners, appear over the horizon, approach quietly through the grass.

That weekend we kept on going. For a few hours it felt like shift work – grab some sleep while you can – and after a while it all began to mix together so that you didn't know if this was the same veggie burger you were still eating from a minute ago or if you'd gone out all night, had a nap and then come back and got another veggie burger. Moments gripped onto you but it was difficult to put them back in the right order.

Sunday was the last night. When the bands had all finished we met at The Place and headed to the top fields, still singing Stevie Wonder ('My baby loves me, my baby neeeeeds me') and into a wide low tent with proper pianos-and-hands-in-the-air house music playing. Chubby man behind the decks, wrecked and elated. We were all together – me, Mandy, Stella, Luigi and Kate, Al, Jenny – and we moved through and towards the front. It was stumbly underfoot, bare earth and dropped bottles and cups, and I moved my feet up-across-and-down with each step, landing flat-footed, like a puppet. The place was crowded, soft and jostling, and then we reached a little clearing and stopped. We faced the front and all closed our eyes, I think, rave-bathing for a few seconds before the dancing properly started. Luigi passed one of his bags of MDMA around, Al put his rucksack down and Mandy piled her coat on top, and we danced, in twos and threes and singles but all together. My cheeks ached from smiling and the tips of my fingers buzzed.

'Oh my girls!' Stella shouted at me and Mandy, tears in her eyes. She started laughing, a relaxed laugh, slow and swaying. She hugged me, gripped on like a koala-bear toy, and Mandy scooped her arms around us both. I wanted to dance and I spun around, took a hand from each of them, lifted up their arms so we were a tripod. We all spun round, tried to keep hold, and then we danced again, kept dancing. Luigi and Kate were a few feet away, copying each other's turns and claps, and Al and Jenny were whooping at the DJ. I swung down from my waist, my head upside down, backs of my fingers touching the flattened grass. I felt my back stretching, my neck stretching, and I wiggled my toes, wiggled my fingers.

Then I stood up, tall and inhaling, and Francine was a few yards over to the right. We hadn't seen her all day. She was just there, dancing, further into the tent than we were so she must have been there already when we came in. She didn't dance like some zen robot, she was fully going for it. She pogoed to the bangingest of the bass and then she would do that daft ravey skipping dance, side to side, with her arms moving in time. I watched her and saw that she was watching the people around her, eating them up with her eyes.

I took the baggy out of Luigi's back pocket and shuffled through to Francine. When she saw me her eyes widened in delight. I felt so happy I didn't know what to do with my face.

'MDMA!' I yelled over the music, and held the baggy open between us, at belly height. I realised I hadn't even seen her standing up until now. She licked her finger, aimed it wiggling into one corner of the bag, and I had a moment to take her in. She was a little bit shorter than me, she was still wearing her dungarees and her hair was still in thick plaits although they were quite frayed now. I looked at the froth of loose strands, at her eyebrows and lashes, her nose, her ears, her tongue which stuck out for a second when she winced at the taste of the powder. I gave her my hipflask so she could wash it down and took another scoop of the MDMA for myself, then I sipped some schnapps and fed her one more glug. It fell down her chin because she was smiling so widely.

From where we were I could see people's faces looking towards the DJ booth. There were arms waving and people jumping but mainly it was one person swaying, one person bouncing, one rocking side to side, another back and forth. More and more layers were adding to the music and more and more people were smiling, heads back, and more arms raised up. One woman leaned against a huge tent post, drank some water, eyes closed. A man with long hair in a high ponytail was singing along, although there were no words in the song. His friend, right next to him, was clapping in encouragement. I saw Luigi, his sweatshirt tied round his head, whoop-whooping with one finger bouncing in the air. Mandy and Stella were in a waltzing hug, Kate was swaying, her arms were fronds above her head. Jenny was sitting on some big black box, a generator maybe, and Al was doing his little boxer shuffle – arms pulled up in front of him and shoulders tick-tocking.

Francine was still right next to me but she was back into her dancing too, eyes gliding around, always smiling. I moved back to the others and I don't think she noticed. She had her arms out straight to the side, about to take off.

'Did you see Francine dancing?' I said to Mandy, but she didn't hear. She put her hands on top of my head, slid them down over my hair, ears, cheeks, neck, shoulders, and we danced together again. A couple of songs later I looked over and I couldn't see Francine anymore. Sometime after that the music stopped and people began to cluster and desert.

Luigi and Kate took Al to the Stone Circle, but we went to the Dead Zone again. The back of an aeroplane had been stuck into the ground and we climbed in – there was a woman selling nasty vodka jelly shots and a man gave us his blanket to sit under while he played us songs on his little keyboard, sang bits of lyrics that he couldn't properly remember. We paid him in schnapps and applause, and snuggled together, and after a while he got distracted and wandered off, left us under his blanket.

At around nine that morning we got back to the tents. Luigi and Al and Kate were sitting all on one hay bale, with a duvet over their shoulders. Al was in the middle, whispering 'Squeegee Luigi, squeegee Luigi,' tickling Luigi just below his ribs. They were all jitters and sleepy elation. There was a tent-sized, tent-shaped patch of flattened yellowed grass where Francine's tent had been.

'Where did Francine go?' I said. The three of them looked at me.

'She left, I think, she's gone. She left. We didn't see her go.' This was Al, sounding wistful.

'Should we go and look for her?' said Kate. I couldn't tell if she was taking the piss. It's not like we'd lost a kitten or a toddler.

'Do you think she's okay?' I asked, and Mandy frowned.

'We don't know anyone to ask,' she said. 'We don't know her surname or anyone she knows.'

Al made that 'duh duh duhhh' mystery cliffhanger sound, his eyes wide.

'She doesn't know anyone, that's why,' said Luigi. 'Anyway it's Monday morning. She's gone home.'

Jenny looked at the empty patch and said, 'She's got my head-torch.'

We packed up ourselves an hour or so later, after Al had been to get us warm porridge and cups of tea from the caravan. Everything was slow and heavy. We dragged our stuff to the car park, and didn't mention Francine. Apart from, kind of, at one point when Luigi tried to help Stella with her bag, a holdall which kept slipping off her shoulder as she dragged her broken wheelie suitcase behind her with a tent balanced on top of it. 'I'm fine,' she told him, and kept on dragging, and he raised his eyebrows. In the car when Mandy offered me a cigarette I told her, 'I'm fine,' and we both started laughing, and Stella did too, and that was that.

Except now it's a year later and here we are back at Glastonbury. Luigi and Kate broke up and neither of them came this time, but Mandy has brought Tom with her and Bernice decided to join us as well. We're camping in the same spot as last year and there's room for another tent to slot into our circle. We agreed that there was no sense in cramming in too close. But it's Friday already and it's still only us here.

WILGEFORTIS

Eley Williams

Jenny had no idea how to pronounce *Wilgefortis* correctly but she would certainly give it her best shot at any given moment. This was her current thinking on the matter – surely it could not be *wilge* as in *bilge* and it must be four syllables rather than three: *Wil-guh-for-tis*. St. Wilgefortis was Jenny's favourite saint.

According to her research, achieved in snatched moments during boring maths lessons with her phone beneath the desk, St. Wilgefortis is also occasionally known as 'Uncumber'. In Holland, she's called 'Ontkommer' too. Google Translate implies that the word *ontkommer* roughly approximates to *escaper*. In France, Wilgefortis is known as Débarras. This translates as *riddance*.

Just as Wilgefortis was Jenny's favourite saint, *philtrum* was Jenny's favourite word. At times of stress she had developed a habit of pressing a finger into that natural depression between her nose and her upper lip and once she learned that there was a word for that depression she found that she was forever repeating it in her head – *philtrum philtrum philtrum*. It comes from the Greek, literally meaning *love charm*.

You may have heard of *philtrum* as it's a real boon for Scrabble players. You may have heard of St. Wilgefortis because she is depicted in religious art and iconography as sporting a thick, lustrous beard.

Thinking about favourite saints, and beards, and words, Jenny locked the bathroom door behind her.

'You shouldn't listen to what Vanessa says,' her best friend Anna had told her earlier that afternoon as they stood in the queue for lunch.

'But do I? Do I have one?' Jenny had asked. She did not like seeing her friend try to lie so as she spoke she kept her eyes fixed on the school canteen's fridges. The remaining sandwiches were tuna and cucumber. The very worst of the worst of the worst. After four years at school Jenny had trained herself to recognise tuna and cucumber sandwiches from the furthest limits of the queue by the little blue cartoon fish on the corner of the packaging. The cartoon fish gave Jenny the thumbs-up, illustrating that the tuna was dolphin-friendly.

'You can only really see it when you stand in profile,' Anna replied, hopping from foot to foot.

'But I'm always standing in profile for somebody.'

'It's just downy, Jenny. Don't worry about it.'

It's just downy. It's just puppy-fat. You are somewhere between a duckling and a young dog, Jenny. Don't worry about it.

Jenny nodded. Then she put down her tray, walked from the lunch-hall and went out into the hot July rain to the bus-stop. The words *downy downy downy downy* played in her ears all the way home, knelling in a new headache for her. She placed her finger on her upper lip and prayed to St. Wilgefortis. *Philtrum philtrum philtrum.*

Once home Jenny went straight up the stairs and into the bathroom where she switched on the light and watched all the surfaces come back bright and brash at her. It took one blink – one breath, four steps and a single semi-slip in her socks to get to the medicine cabinet; as she pulled its mirror-fronted doors open, Jenny watched her reflection halve itself straight down the middle. The cabinet was overstuffed and some plasters and an emery board fell down into the sink straight from the shelves. She picked them back up and lined them according to size next to her mother's special menthol toothpaste. She put the emery board beneath them as an underline as if for emphasis. *Phil-trum*, *phil-trum*, the dripping tap seemed to say. Jenny began searching the cabinet. She flicked the brown glass bottles and the sides of the paper packets with her fingernail. She caught the side of a pumice stone with her thumb and her teeth went on edge at the texture of it, its capacity to crumble. You are somewhere between a duckling and a young dog. You have the potential to eat bread and to fetch things.

There have been sculptures and carvings of St. Wilgefortis dating from the 11th century. She resembles the familiar crucified Christ in the iconography – narrow-faced and looking down with pained benevolence from the cross. Long hair with a centre parting and a beard down to the chest. The full-length flowing tunic is the giveaway. In later paintings of St. Wilgefortis, this is a beautiful embroidered dress covered in flowers and she wears soft blue slippers.

According to their boxes, all the aspirins in Jenny's house were 'dissolve in the mouth.' Boiled sweets and fudge are sold as 'melt in the mouth' in her school canteen – no doubt there are rules about why these two product descriptions are phrased ever so slightly differently. Jenny imagined such rules are set out by some man working in Trading Standards wearing a brown suit, a green tie and *Ipcress Files*-style glasses.

Why would the dip between your upper lip and nose be named

after the Greek for *love charm*? Maybe it's related to Cupid and his bow. Again, according to Jenny's phone and its articles from every corner of the internet: 'each unborn child has an angel teaching them all of the wisdom in the world while they are in utero. The angel lightly taps the infant's upper lip before birth to silence the infant from telling all the secrets in the universe to the humans who reside in it.' The grammar of this sentence makes Jenny frown and tap her philtrum. She presses a little harder.

On her tiptoes by the sink, Jenny found her father's old leather wash-bag behind a row of gummed-up bottles of cough medicine, all four years out of date. The wash-bag had a broad metal zip, like a pencil case. She took it from the cabinet and felt its pleasing bulkiness. She unzipped it, re-zipped it, unzipped it once more. She enjoyed the *allyup* sound this made, bouncing against the quiet and round ceramic angles of the bathroom. Her mother's wash-bag was covered in flowers and its zip didn't quite make the same noise.

Jenny lay down on the cool floor of the bathroom and upended her father's washbag. For some reason her father had kept a button and a pound coin in there which she put carefully to one side, away from the stray pills and puff of cotton wool. She stacked the small square foil packets she found there into a little house-of-cards arrangement. She unscrewed the white bottle of contact-lens fluid and smelt it.

It had been raining all day. It was a cloying, muggy July rain that steamed on its way down because of the heat – Jenny could see drops of it from the floor in the reflection of the cabinet doors, making wet pinstripes against the window. It was a seething rain that fell sideways, italic. It had made the tree leaves stink on the walk from the bus stop.

It had been the sound of the rain against the maths lesson windows that had almost made her miss Vanessa's comment. 'At least I don't have a moustache,' she had hissed at Jenny across her desk. Vanessa's eyebrows had risen and fallen as she said this and then she had looked back at her calculator as if nothing had happened, as if the world hadn't just stalled. Jenny, dazed, found herself blanking out the statement and just staring at Vanessa's eyebrows. They were unsettling, fascinating – little flattish chevrons of hair stark against the smoothness of her forehead. Jenny knew that the word for the skin between the eyebrows is *glabella*. An ugly word. Maybe a prettier word than *Wilgefortis*, however. Jenny wondered whether any girls in the world were named *Glabella*. The evolutionary reason for eyebrows, Jenny knew, is to catch the sweat from our brows, that they provide little weir-gates of fluff to sluice away the worst effects of salt and moisture. But why not then have entirely hairy foreheads? Why do our scalps not reach down all the way to our eyes? Presumably because our brains would overheat if they did not whirr away under that little window of bare, skylight-plane flesh.

Jenny had then realised she was touching her upper lip and had her mouth fully open.

Jenny picked out her father's long-abandoned straight razor from the floor. It was made of wood and metal and had his initials worked into it along the side. She unfolded it in the way she had seen actors do in Westerns.

When she started secondary school, Jenny could remember feeling her potential opening up in her throat, in her chest, in her head. She felt it physically in her hands as she walked into her first classroom. She forced the fists that she did not even know she had made to uncurl, finger by finger. She now reckoned it must be some kind of excess of this new energy that caused all the other things to happen to her body that were beginning to preoccupy her and her classmates: changes in body shape, hair, skin, new confusions and obtrusions and outwardlinesses as childhood and its familiarities were left behind.

Vanessa had always managed to pick up and comment upon every one of these instances before even Jenny had a chance to notice them herself.

In her bathroom, Jenny stood up with the razor. She closed the cabinet doors so she could see her reflection again.

Jenny didn't really believe in God or saints, but she enjoyed praying to Wilgefortis. It was not so much a prayer as a *hello*. She imagined Wilgefortis didn't get many prayers sent her way. Jenny wondered whether anyone ever found Wilgefortis' face miraculously appearing in clouds or rocky outcrops or similar but, because of her beard, mistook the vision for that of Jesus Christ. Jenny had once found a crisp that – in the right light, to a very gullible person – looked a bit like what she imagined Jesus Christ or Wilgefortis to look like. It was a stain baked into the yellow of the crisp. You could sort of make out the eyes, the hair, the beard. She considered selling the crisp to a credulous relic-hunter who might believe the pattern of the crisp was significant. On a whim, she had uploaded a photo of the crisp and run it through a face-comparison website. The website had come up with Ralph Fiennes, Robert Redford and Clea DuVall as possible matches to the face found there. Knowing this, Jenny couldn't then sell the Jesus Christ-Wilgefortis crisp in good faith.

Jenny listened to the sounds of the water-heater in the airing cupboard next door. The tick of the heater came almost exactly in time with a pulse in her throat. She watched the pulse. As she watched, either her pulse or the water-heater changed pace.

Philtrum, philtrum.

Jenny watched the mist made by her breath glaze the medicine cabinet doors. Backwards in the mirror, her father's initials on the razor handle almost spelt out a rude word. A question mark of her hair sprung out of its fastening across her forehead.

She didn't blame Vanessa, really. Jenny found she was laid low by all kinds of things nowadays. She had cried twice because of half-caught news features she heard on the radio – a team of thieves had taken to hacking off cows' legs and leaving them to die in the field because it was easier to run off with just one joint of meat than a whole cow. Ancient, priceless ruins of Mesopotamia had been unwittingly ground up and packed into sandbags by soldiers in parts of Iraq. Hearing both these things, Jenny had not-prayed to Wilgefortis and pressed her philtrum.

Downy downy downy. In the maths classroom, as Vanessa looked back to her calculator, the birds had left the tree outside the window in one slow movement, unhurried because of the rain. They had seemed to Jenny as if they were moving in slow motion – sluggish, literally under the weather, shouldering the clouds upward in the wet summer warmth. Jenny thought the whole of July had reeked of static heat. Vanessa's words still hot in her ears, Jenny was suddenly aware that she was covered in sweat. With one twist of her shoulders, she imagined that she could wring herself out.

Jenny wondered if she could grow a full moustache before she died. She screwed up her eyes at her reflection and wondered whether she could pull off a handlebar.

Jenny used her father's badger-bristle shaving brush and some yellow soap to build up a thick lather. She caught sight of herself in the mirror one last time and gave her reflection a shy, sure smile.

PEEP HOLE

Leone Ross

He opens his eyes at 9.17am and lies half-asleep, aware of small pains, of the middle-aged kind. The pain gnaws his knuckle bone, just where he balanced himself to fuck her far longer than he should have, and it blooms in the space between his shoulder and earlobe. He's slept at a bad angle to accommodate her.

It's the first time he's stayed all night at hers and he's hungry, despite the cannelloni and pumpkin lasagne and stale garlic bread they'd ordered after the sex. The later he eats these days, the hungrier he is on waking. His lover surprised him by ordering the food and paying for it. She does him few favours. It's he who comes to bestow favours, when she calls for him, like flesh takeaway.

He'd arrived late last night, after drinks with old friends – ex-lovers really, but friends too, of a fashion. They share enough aesthetic tastes to hold a conversation, and enough political beliefs to avoid a fight. One is his ex-student, a tall glossy brother of the type that never fits into chairs. The ex-student used to pat his shoulder after sex, an alarmingly avuncular motion given his youth, and then slot himself around him, pulling his prone arm up and back, around his neck. Lying like that made him feel like a snail on its side, or something fallen out of a jar. The other friend drinking Wray & Nephew with them was the kind of woman who laughed too hard, who'd be pulling up her skirts in the loo for you at the slightest suggestion, bruising her knees like overripe fruit.

His present lover, she who owns this bed and this small, empty orange apartment, has no interest in his heart. It's taken him several months to accept this: that there will be no yearning for him. He imagines his penis unlocking itself from the ego, like a brown, iron hinge. Still, at 64, he is pleased to have the core strength necessary for her demands, even if it means waking up slightly beaten, like an egg, and not coming over all that much so he has recovery time. She insists he enter her very slowly because that's the way her body works best and so he does, one eye closed, like threading a needle. He's tried pushing past her boundaries twice, desperate to plunge, but she ended up sore and bad-tempered, drying out on the end of his cock, a deeply unpleasant sensation.

It was necessary to forgive a woman for not loving you even when you fucked her well, because otherwise things curdled and rotted and howled.

Last night they'd agreed he would stay over and wake up when he wished. It seemed silly to force them both out of bed, competing for baths, hurrying into the urban dank, a red sunrise, together, into the smell of city hours before it was necessary. They discussed it sleepily, after the fuck. His wife – and there was a wife – would have called it a whole other level of betrayal. She was a real person, his wife, not something he *had,* like a sideboard or a new computer. She glowed, generally, and was all of herself and she'd be furious to know this had morphed from a one-night stand into a just-stay-on-and-shut-the-door-hard-behind-you thing.

His wife is away for three days, and so.

Stay, his lover said drowsily. *There's bits in the fridge. Just have anything you want. I'll do a pot of coffee before I go.* She is the co-owner of a small, lime-coloured café, everything as full-fat and carnivorous as she can make it: sugary, creamy, bloody, vulgar. Huge portions, dumped on plates. Duty annoys her, and restraint, unless it's him, sipping her clit. They don't use condoms, because she has a coil and he a vasectomy and she likes bare-back sex, likes pointing out that they're fucking raw and unprotected in the middle of it all, giggling.

So many levels of betrayal.

Last night he found out that she's a neat sleeper, curled on her clearly-delineated side of the bed, still as death until the quiet beeping of an alarm. She slunk off the mattress, a trickle of shadow he could hear bumping around in the dark, careful not to disturb him, the bitter smell of coffee pumping. He'd drifted back to sleep, momentarily surprised she was so considerate.

Awake for the second time now, he sits up, a simple plan in mind: he will take a piss, drink the promised coffee, maybe nose through her silent books and DVDs, then head out for early lunch. It's a bit much, using her spatula, her crockery, doing the washing up after. Too domestic, too... intimate, although he will enjoy wandering through her place naked and alone. He needn't scrub his nooks and crannies as hard as he usually does before he leaves; his whole family is away at a Portuguese spa retreat. His wife said she might let his teenage daughters have a little wine in the evenings, and he'd laughed and said he was sure they'd done *that* by now, given the stream of anxious, preening boys filing through his large house.

They'd done well.

Yes: a piss, a coffee, lunch, like that.

Except the kitchen is cold on his bare backside and there is no coffee anywhere he looks, certainly not Jamaican Blue Mountain, which she mentioned last night, not even so-so instant coffee. The humming fridge is clean and empty, except for a water filter and a hunk of fresh cheddar. No milk. He shakes his head.

On his way back down the tiny hallway to the bedroom, for reasons he doesn't understand, he glances through the peephole in the front door. Perhaps it is a habit; a way to glance at the outside before he re-enters it. Perhaps...

And there is a woman standing quietly in front of the door, staring at the door, swaying in the breeze, like a lamp.

The man jerks back.

Even considering it years later, his response had been strange. Most people would have yelled out a greeting and opened the door, readying themselves to take the package or the message or to brush off a charity call. Flowers. Look at the water meter. Pleasant greetings.

But, no: he recoils, hushed, and still. There is something about the swaying woman that alarms him immediately, that makes him take his face away from the door as if it's burning. She might have been a shop mannequin; he has the impression of unnatural smoothness, imagines the joins attaching her plastic arms to her shoulders, her no-nippled chest, the beige swathe of her, flesh-coloured, they call it, annoying his wife, *whose flesh* she says, proud to be an ally in so many fights.

The man takes a deep breath of the air inside the apartment and chides himself. Perhaps it's the stillness of this space unsettling him: no children's voices, no clatter of heels, no lover moaning; whatever the case, he must look through the peephole, again. He chuckles at himself; there is no smooth woman standing at the door. She was a speck in his eye, a shadow, the movement of a bird or a tree.

He traces the door with his fingertip.

His lover has an altar in the hallway. Candles, encouraging mantras, statues, a beet-purple cloth. *Keep moving towards your greatness*, one slip of paper says, and he's offended by her banality. Is that a book about astrology, on the shelf behind?

Come now.

He puts his eye to the peephole, so determined, he can't focus; adjusts his vision in time to see the top of the woman's head. The shine of her hair is too glossy to be a mannequin, the shine on her forehead too much of human oil to be anything other than real, the crown of her head swaying, the yellow-brown of her scalp aflame in the sudden winter sunshine.

He is conscious of his nakedness, as if he's exposed himself to her. Why is she just standing there, real and alive, while people are trying to go about their business? He supposes there could be any number of reasons. *Open the door*, he thinks. Perhaps she's already knocked and he just didn't hear it, yes, he's relieved to think it: she is one of those people who flit like bats and make so little sound, you don't notice them. Vampiric. A soucouyant. Duppy. Fairie-people. His second daughter is a slip of a thing: sometimes he doesn't see her, curled in an armchair or waiting for a load of washing. *You always miss me, dad*, she says. She adores him; he is a good daddy.

His hesitance makes less sense than the woman's mute rocking. The top of her head breaks his heart. The centre of it, the gleaming scalp, the sullen sunshine. Is she old? Cold? He's unsure. She will be gone soon, surely. A religious ecstatic, pausing for breath between handout tracts? Asthmatic. Perhaps she needs help, and he is just standing here bare-footed, his dangling balls cold and ridiculous.

I'm coming, I'm coming, he mutters low, appalled by his lack of strength, of volume, by the weak winter sunshine sinning on the hallway floor, shuffling backward in the narrow corridor, past his lover's neatly-hung coats in lemon and peach, something he liked about her from the beginning, these fruit choices against her dark skin, her Blackness warming the colours, like rich soil. The first time he reached up inside her red shirt and weighed her breast, rubbed a full palm across that skin, he gasped, it had been so long since he touched skin like his own. Was the woman at the door Black? Her hair was black, perhaps she was Asian, Indian. Surely she wasn't still there, clutching a Bible or her chest, but if she was, he had a duty to help.

Back in the bedroom, the torn bed reminds him of himself, stooped between his lover's thighs, lapping, holding on as she rides his face, grunting in frustration. *It takes me a long time,* she says and he can't find his briefs, then finds them in the next inflamed moment. There is the sound of a gull somewhere and rustling in the branches of the tree outside his lover's balcony. A boy calls out, sweet-voiced, in the distance. *Dada*, he says, the sound of him plaited.

The man drags on his jeans, wrong-legged then right, and his hoodie. The heart of him has not stopped banging. *Where are you going,* he asked his wife when she said she'd be gone for three days. *My old friend Mary*, she said, *the girls are on a school trip, you'll be all alone*. He can't remember the last time he saw her pale throat in moonlight.

Surely the woman is gone, but if not, he has only taken minutes, he can still help her.

Back in the hall, he applies his eye to the peephole. The icy shock of her presence startles him, still standing in the same position, eyes down. Perhaps she is meditating. Perhaps someone died here, and she is paying respects. He's seen bunches of cheap roses and daisies on the local roads, commemorating a boy struck off his bicycle; a stabbing. He presses his ear to the wood. Might she be crying? Her nimbus skull. Why does she trouble him so, with her calm? Let her be. Perhaps this isn't as strange as it seems. He needs another person's opinion. The air around him bends and yawns. He's not seen anyone in a million hours, give or take. There's his spittle and breath on the door, where his mouth pressed, and eye pressed. Did his lover bathe before she left? He hadn't heard the sound of a bath running. She'd sat up abruptly, no need for an alarm, snapped on the lights, waking him, not even a good morning his way. He wanted to force her between his thighs, take a deep breath of their stink, her long, pink tongue in nasty places. For him. For his penis, bunched like a piece of dank wool. He'd managed to go back to sleep with a pillow over his head to block the light, momentarily surprised she was so inconsiderate.

Who is concerned to please *him*, who sends him roses for his pains, who worries after his well-being these days or ever has? He remembers a dinner lady, when he was small, giving him white sugar sandwiches. The crunch against his teeth.

Why should he be concerned for the woman at the peephole or moved to save her? There is a lacy cobweb in the eaves above his head; he wouldn't expect such a thing of his lover, who seems so house-proud and puts lotion on her feet and shines her own shoes, but she's a busy woman. Might he get her a cleaner? He finds the idea inexplicably arousing, what he might do for her. She pulls away when she's close to orgasm but can't; says it's harder for her to cum because she doesn't love him; he pulls her back onto his cock, eventually feels her spasm and squeal and speak in tongues. *Jesus Christ, you kill me when I do, though*, she says.

He must look out the peephole again. Even if he owes the stranger nothing, he can bear witness. He can give her his eye. Would you die alone, standing at some random door, your forehead pressed against it?

She has moved, ever so slightly. The head is less bowed, he can see more of her face. The eyebrows are thin and fine, the nose beautifully sculpted, even at this fish-bowl angle. He thinks of a card series his older daughter liked when she was nine: fish-bowl kitties and puppies and giraffes, was there a gorilla, a koala? His caramel children. When he took them to nursery runs when they were little, the mums at the gate remarked on the shades of them, perfectly mixed and seasoned, their eyes on his own frothy, chocolate goodness, drink him up like a macchiato, they might. The longing of these gossiping women for their own caramel babies in prams, it made him ill. All he'd done was fall in love with one honeyed blonde, his wife, a person, a singular, his first. It wasn't a habit. But he felt part of a conspiracy, creating this honey, caramel, chocolate household. It was different here in his lover's bed, their Black hands together on her blue and yellow sheets, he sniffing her pillows like a puppy, this meadow of light.

Paranoia makes him shudder with a new thought: his wife has sent a spy! But of course not, she would never do such a thing, too dignified, too busy to be bothered. *A nice white girl*, his family said, and from each of them the sentence meant something different, depending on which word you emphasised.

There is a skittering, scraping sound and he applies his left eye, letting his heart fall away. He cannot tell what race she is, perhaps it is the peephole that has rendered her unidentifiable, or the weather, her flawless skin exposing no cultural marker, as if that part of his brain has been wrenched away. He is distracted by the circle of the peephole, its blurred golden edges. He can see buildings behind her head into a ceaseless distance, why, it seems the whole of the city is in the peephole, smoothed and undulating. Finally, he knows what she is: no drug dealer, no postman, no one selling gym memberships or hearts, she is no lion-tamer, she has come with no fruit or skin, no promises. She is a kaleidoscope, changing the patterns of the universe, giving him an insectoid gaze.

She looks up and straight into his eyes.

He flings himself backwards, as if she's driven nails into his throat.

She is quite insane.

He must get away. Get out of this house. He's tall and strong; all he needs to do is fling open the door. He's run out of patience. He's starving. As he backs up the hallway, he can smell coffee and more than that: cinnamon, cardamom, nutmeg. There is a newly-baked warm loaf in the kitchen, just for him, bleeding butter. He blinks, mouth awash. Each time he leaves, his lover follows him to the door, and presses her mouth against his and they laugh in their completed lust but they are really laughing so as not to cry or to make any space for him to ask for anything else.

The woman outside is insane, but he can walk right through her. His hands and the back of his neck sting at the thought of her falling forward, her skin on him. But it will only take seconds to cast her away. He strides into the living room, retrieves his shoes and socks where he first pulled them off. Did his lover undress him there, when he arrived last night? He can't remember. His skin trembles. There are parts of his body he only lets special people touch: his children's hands in his spine, arms wrapped around the backs of his calves, when they were small, clinging to his knees when his knees were strong, everyone squealing and laughing. What he might be for them...

Around him, the flat cools, the thing at the door scratches. Rage barrels him back past the altar, and he applies his fists to the door, surprised to hear the bark coming from his throat.

Get away from the door, now, bitch get away! I shall come out!

He imagines the woman springing backwards, her mad, soft body cowed by the force of his fists and his strong voice. People think things about him that are not true, they have since he was little: that he's more certain, more calculating, more dangerous than he really is, a panther, his wife likes to say, and he wants to strike her down for all the years she's said it. He's had women before, who have greedily enjoyed sex, but this lover, she fucks like an angel. One afternoon she sprouted feathers on top of her shoulders, no larger than hummingbird wings, and he stroked them with his thumb. When she does orgasm, she is a great, stickle-backed forest grappling him, a river breaking its banks, bubbling into the margins of the bed, rushing and foaming.

Get away, he cries, beating the door, *you're not here for me! There's nothing here to see! I'm not* – he wants to say his name but finds it stuck in his throat, along with the lack of guilt, thick like butter, no, he doesn't give a damn, he wants what he wants, is entitled to it, his need to feel a dark head at night; we should all have what we want.

He wants sugar, crumbled on bread and lard, sandy against his lips.

He looks through the peephole. Her huge eyes stare back, unblinking. He cannot see if she has eyelashes. Or if she's human. The sound of his fists, his masculine command, none of it means anything to her. She is inexorable. Is she nothing more than a disembodied head, and if he confronts her, will the sight of her split his brain apart?

He sits on the floor, knees up, his ear against the hard door and the thing outside scratches; he thinks she is using the toes of one of her feet below the letterbox. Does she come every day? How could his lover have left and not warned him?

The flap of the letterbox.

It will be, he approximates, at the level of her belly button. He sucks his own tongue. Bites the inside of his cheek. Scratching, she's scratching and he's wet his decent underwear, can smell his own urine. What's for breakfast?

The belly of the thing, through the flap.

His wife's belly is flat and soft. There are three blood-coloured dots on it, he's not sure why. His lover's belly is the biggest part of her. The first time he slid his fingers into her jeans and down towards her pussy he realised he'd have to work around and *under* her belly, to get access. She'd shifted – uncomfortably? – she was human, after all – waiting on him to work it out.

He slides his fingers up and towards the letterbox. Trembling fingers. Trembling feet, toes clenching. The flap is large enough for quite a big package. The flap will allow for his whole hand, his whole fist. The sinking of fingers into kaleidoscope flesh. Whatever it takes. She must stand away from the door. She must fly away into the afternoon. She must stop seeing all of him through wood and concrete. She must let him past.

There are mutterings, singing in other apartments. Shadows are oily. The cry of a fox. His fingers slither. He can't see what he's doing. The early dark of winter. How long has he been here, pissing, begging? He must end it now. Fingers in her belly. It will be an easy, necessary destruction, a relief.

Disembowel the soft things.

Clip, click, his hand at the slot, pushing up, nails pushing through the soft, feathery lips of the door, under the sharp flap, if you weren't careful you could cut yourself. Click, clip. The sound of her soft belly, sizzling.

The sound of a key.

His hand, grasping nothing, teeth are chalk, he is crying, the cold night rushing in on him, the door pulled away from his grasp, reeling forwards, off his heels, onto his knees, the way his lover is sometimes, how they bow between each other's thighs, what glory! She is surprised to see him there, gasping, her dark hands fluttering, calling him by his name, asking him how come he still here, did you sleep all day?

Did you sleep.

FOUND GIRLS

Kirsty Logan

Early Shift

Alice's lecture is good. She knows it. She put in the hours, perfected her script, searched out all the best quotations. Her points are smart and original, but not too original, so the students will still be able to pass their exams. She goes fast enough that it never gets boring, but not so fast that the students can't keep up.

But it's more than that. She's a performer. When she steps, apparently without thinking, from one side of the lecture hall to the other, she feels the eyes of every student in the place following her. They even mirror her body language: if she tilts her head, so do they. If she tucks a loose blonde strand behind her ear, suddenly they're all bothered by having their hair in their faces.

The course is Gender, Work, and the Body as Performance. It studies, according to the course catalogue, *the ways in which the process of the creation of gender and/or sexual identities are objectified and commodified in a capitalist society, and how this is used to de-personalise those engaged in this process.* It's always a popular one. Alice doesn't know if it's because of the inclusion of the words 'sex' and 'body', or because of her. Or maybe it's that eighteen year-old undergrads are genuinely interested in the creation of gender and/or sexual identities.

The clock hits the hour, Alice sets the reading, and the students start to file out. She collects her papers and shakes back her hair. It's a thrill, to perform. To have them all look at her and listen to her. To have her work seep into so many brains, to change them. She'll never know how often what happens in this room will replay in the students' minds after this day. The smallest thing could affect the rest of their lives. There's a strange power in that, and Alice likes it.

She heads for the door, and there he is. Of course. She always forgets his name. Something basic, Biblical. John. Mark. Luke. Not even a fun one like Zillah or Moab.

'Dr Alice?' the student says. She's not a doctor and he shouldn't be using her first name, but she doesn't say anything, just smiles in a vague and benign way. 'Dr Alice, I need to run my essay by you? I'll come by your office after hours? Tomorrow? I'll email it to you before and you can read it and we can discuss it?'

Everything is a statement, a demand, but his voice goes up at the end as if it's a question. Alice finds it deeply fucking irritating, but then it's hard to know whether that's just because she finds John/Mark/Zillah deeply fucking irritating. He's said his piece, already turning to go.

'No,' she says. She knows she sounds harsh, but she has learned that *no* is a complete sentence. She has also learned that this student, this man – all students, all men – will require further sentences to explain it. Still, baby steps. The students will learn boundaries eventually. She gets paid for what she gets paid for.

'What, Dr Alice?' the student says, and he's smiling, as if perhaps she's joking, as if it's inconceivable that she'd work only the hours she's meant to work. 'I thought you said no?'

'Students can visit me in office hours,' says Alice, and she thinks *cheerful robot*: Smile and repeat, smile and repeat. 'I don't have any office hours tomorrow. Students may not send tutors their work to check before deadline. You may speak to me, briefly, about your essay before the next class comes in.'

That evening, John emails Alice his essay, along with a reminder that he'll come by after office hours tomorrow.

But Alice doesn't check her email in the evenings. Like most academics these days – like most people these days – she has more than one job. More than one identity. She does one of the jobs to support the other. But lately she's not sure which is the real job and which is the support.

* * *

'Harder!' says Dorothy. 'Give me another thirty!' She can see already that the client can't manage another thirty – her arms are shaking like fuck, if she tries another push-up she'll smack right down on her face; Dorothy will have to be ready to catch her in a way that looks professional, safe, like it's part of the training – but she's said it now, so she has to stick with it. 'Thirty and done,' she adds, trying not to make it sound like a concession. 'You can do it! I believe in you!'

Then she catches a glimpse of herself in the wall-to-wall mirrors and rethinks her words of soft, cheerleader-esque encouragement. Standing there with her hands on her hips, hard muscles gleaming under the bright lights, she looks intimidating. But that's sort of the point. Personal trainers shouldn't be soft. They shouldn't be encouraging. They shouldn't be your goddamned mother. Or maybe some of them can be, in some places, but not here in this gym: the thunk of weights, the reek of sweat, the occasional and entirely non-ironic roar of effort. Everyone has matching Lycra ensembles. Everyone has a protein shake. Everyone has visible veins. People who want mothers go elsewhere.

'Go harder! Push it!' she says instead. The words hang in the chilled, sweat-heavy air of the gym and Dorothy regrets them a little. They sound weirdly sexual. But there's nothing she can do about that now. The client is halfway now; only another fifteen to go.

Dorothy sees herself in the mirror. She holds her stance so her thighs show their power. She allows her arm muscles to tense and swell. She sees others glance over, both men and women. It's not that they want her – they want to *be* her. They want to be better than her. Bigger, stronger. They won't be, but that's the promise her body makes: do what I say and you can be what I am.

She should be counting down the client's last few push-ups. Any moment now she's going to face-plant on the mat. Dorothy looks at herself in the mirror, trying to resist the urge to raise her arms up above her head and shriek a victory sound at the ceiling. 'If you want to *be* the best,' Dorothy finds herself saying, 'you have to *beat* the best.' She grins to herself as she says it, wondering if it sounds at all familiar to the client. There's no danger if it does: when she says it later, she'll be wearing a mask.

Dorothy helps the client up and slaps her on the back, congratulating her on going harder, then sends her off to the shower room.

Dorothy has a full schedule today. She barely gets enough time for her own workouts, and has to incorporate them into her clients' workouts in the guise of showing them correct form. But she can't slack off. She can't let her body soften or shrink. She can't get soft.

Because it's not about what she says during the personal training sessions. It's not about what she does. It's not even about the programmes she makes for the clients. It's about what they see when they look at her. What she represents, what her body says, the story of it. There's a reason she's the personal trainer with the most clients. Because she knows this is what it's about: who tells a better story with their body.

Late Shift

Wonderland is heading for the door. It's 5am and her shift just finished. She's already thinking of pancakes. With blueberries and syrup. And, fuck it, bacon.

She's changed into her other clothes – not her day shift clothes, her bland trousers and suit jackets, she's not that person now – and though her jeans may be painted-on tight and her lips may be glossed like fancy patisserie, it's still clear she's off shift. Ten minutes ago she was a dancer, and you could pay to look at her, pay to get her to take off her clothes. But now if you look at her too long she'll tell you to fuck right off, and no amount of money will make her say otherwise.

She weaves through the club and to the door, cheekbones buzzing with the too-loud beat of chart rap, sinuses full of the cheap sweet perfume all the girls wear, a huge bottle of it backstage that they all use because they're not wasting their own good stuff from home. She likes backstage – loves it, actually. The camaraderie reminds her of school, the netball team. She played wing defence. They toured around the country on weekends, they stayed in Travelodges and Premier Inns, six to a room to save money, midnight sleepovers bouncing on the beds with family-size bags of Maltesers and scream-laughing at the 30-second free porn previews. Out in the club it's everyone for herself, but backstage the girls share: lipstick, tit tape, notes about who gropes and who tips high.

Wonderland is at the door, she's opening the door, she's almost out –

And there he is. Of course. If she ever knew his name, she doesn't know it now.

'Come see me tomorrow, sugar,' she says, making the words come out slow and soggy because the guys like it that way for reasons she doesn't know but will definitely analyse in a paper at some point. She rests her hand briefly on his chest because she can touch him, of course.

'Let me take you for dinner,' the customer says. Or 'I want to take you on a date,' or 'come out to my car and suck my cock,' – it doesn't matter what he says, she's not listening anyway, the answer will always be the same, and no matter how many empty sugary words she says to him she's really only saying one word, the only word she ever thinks about with customers, because boundaries are important, aren't they, no matter who you are or what your job is people will always try to take more than you need to give, take more than their fair share based on what they're giving you in return, and when she's a stripper she'll strip but that's not who she is right now, and the customer is still trying to speak to her but the door guy is stopping him because he's doing his job, and she's already done her job so she smiles back at the customer and keeps walking outside because whatever he's trying to say to her there's only one answer: *no.*

* * *

'Gale! Gale! Gale!'

The crowd chant as one. And Gale deserves it, she knows she does, because she's done a fucking great show. Is *still* doing a fucking great show.

She loves being a heel. She's been a babyface before, briefly, and it just didn't suit. The pastel outfits. The primped hair. The big pink smile. Nah, she wants this: the black mask, the taunts, the mic drops. The leap off the top ropes, the tornado-spin through the air before slamming into another body. Her name gets chanted a lot more now that she's the villain. And yeah, that might be generous – it's more like a cluster of beer-rowdy blokes yelling something that sounds a bit like her name. But she still climbs to the top rope and raises up her arms, turning her mask-clad face so everyone can see her.

She's up against the favourite face: Darling, a full-moon-breasted redhead with the shtick of being a down-home country girl made of apple pie and fresh cream and roasted corn cobs, y'all, even though she's actually from Sunderland. They've been through the usual moves: the taunts and catcalls into the mic, the slams into the mat, the acrobatic spins and flips. Tonight's narrative is that Gale has been plotting with another heel, Darius the Danger, who's also Darling's ex-boyfriend – that's her ex-boyfriend not in real life, but in the ongoing narrative of the wrestling; though actually Gale suspects maybe in real life too, secretly – to steal Darling's title belt. Gale is meant to win this match, and take Darling's belt, then everyone will boo her and cheer Darling, and then next week there's another storyline about Darling challenging Gale with a good old-fashioned glove-slap; there's an oversized white silk glove in props specifically for this.

Gale likes working with Darling. She communicates well, she's flexible, she has a great line in 'oh shit that hurts please let me go this is all entirely real and you're about to break my arm' faces. Also she doesn't wear heavy perfume at work, which Gale appreciates; when you're going to be getting up close with someone's body, the only way it needs to smell is clean. Darling keeps saying they should go out for drinks sometime, and Gale always agrees, though they both know they won't. They work when they're at work, and outside that, it's a different story. Gale doesn't even know Darling's real name.

Gale is a personal trainer to provide the steady money she needs to be a pro-wrestler. Or she's a pro-wrestler to show off the body she got by training. She's not even sure it matters which way round it is. Both jobs require this body. Both jobs *are* this body. She's walking round the gym, showing her body, making promises with it. She's on the posters advertising shows, she's preening on the top ropes, flexing her lady-guns, which is what she still calls them even though they're bigger than the muscles of every single guy in this crowd. Her body is the story.

She's up on the ropes. She's glancing down to check Darling is ready. She's raising her arms up.

'If you want! To be the BEST! You have to –' She punctuates each word by punching her fist into the air: 'BEAT! THE! BEST!' The end of it is drowned out by the roar of the crowd, and yeah, maybe it's just a bunch of drunk guys looking for an excuse to drink cheap beer and yell out dumb catchphrases, it's not exactly a stadium, she's not exactly a superstar, they don't even know what her face looks like under the mask – but it doesn't matter, none of that matters, because this is her story, the work she's doing with her body, both the hours and months and years she put in to make it look like this, to make it lift and swing and hit like this, but also the work now, the shapes she makes, the ground she covers, how she moves.

Because she knows this is what it's about: who tells a better story with their body.

Home

In a small one-bed flat in the medium-cheap part of the city, two women get home from work. They've put clothes on and taken clothes off. They've performed exactly who everyone expected them to be, depending on where they were and what they were wearing and what everyone around them believed their jobs to be.

'I did something at work,' says Dolly, wrapped in a silky hummingbird-print dressing gown, filling two glasses with wine and putting them on the coffee table, trying each remote in turn before figuring out which one would switch on Netflix. 'Something I shouldn't have done.'

'Which work?' says Al, her glasses on and hair tied back, scooping chicken and broccoli out of the pan and onto two plates. She flops down on the couch and gives Dolly a kiss on the cheek.

'Both.'

'What did you do?'

'I think I broke it.'

'Some equipment?'

'No. Character.'

'What do you mean?'

'I was up there, costume and make-up, full fantasy, standing up on the corner ropes with my arms up, shrieking a victory sound, about to leap off in a tornado spin, the crowd screaming for me. And I just –'

Al speaks through a mouthful of half-chewed broccoli. 'You just what, love?'

'I looked right into the eyes of this guy in the front row, and he looked so ridiculous, his face all scrunched up like he was in pain, and for a second I forgot where I was – like, was he flagging in the middle of an ab workout and I had to gee him on? And I thought – shit, wrong job. You're Gale now, not Dorothy. And I couldn't help it. I laughed.'

'Are you fucking kidding me? I did the exact same thing.'

'You laughed?'

'Yeah, at work. Same thing. Caught this random guy's eye, and forgot who I was for a second. I wasn't Wonderland, but I wasn't Alice either. Maybe I was Al. Or maybe I was someone else again. I thought I was just hanging out with you, fucking around, tipsy and dancing at someone's party. The guy got pissed and thought I was laughing at him.'

'Were you?'

'Yeah, kind of. But it was still a bad idea. Reminded him that I'm not who he wants me to be, and I never will be. None of us are.'

Dolly refills Al's wine glass. 'You know who I want you to be?'

Al takes a sip and gives Dolly a long, sweet-sour wine kiss. 'Who?'

'Whoever the fuck you want to be.'

SKIN

Lena Mohamed

When Mariah dropped her skin to her ankles and stepped carefully out of it, she was pleased to see that it had pooled around her feet in soft gathers. The gold-flecked jelly she submerged it in every night was working.

She still avoided looking at herself in the mirror after shedding, not quite over the sight of her dense, burgundy muscles marbled with white. Still, the sheen on her face when she wore her skin again in the mornings made up for that so, much to Emma's annoyance, she simply moved the mirror from their bedroom to the hall so that she wasn't tempted to sneak a peek.

Settling down to begin her nighttime rituals, she coated the sinews of her hands with the gel, ice cold as it slicked up her arms until she glistened all over. Then, pulling the gauze on so it covered her completely, leaving holes for her eyes, she got into bed.

The news that night was on a slow loop: a spate of skin thefts had taken over the Capital. There were cycles of conversations between people in suits and shiny hair holding newspapers the size of torsos. They speculated: 'I suppose people are desperate for better quality skin and they're driven to unfortunate lengths.'

'These people are monsters. How could they steal another person's skin? What are the victims supposed to do, leave their homes skinless?'

They interviewed the victims in shadows, their grotesque forms too bloody to air on public television. Mariah checked online later to see videos uploaded with their full faces, all thick red meat and stark white eyes bulging – some outraged, some tearful, some begging for their skins to be returned. Mariah thought she may have gone to school with the one called Aliya.

Emma thought she was overreacting, but the next night Mariah slept with her skin on. She brought her nose to her arm to breathe in that salty, chalky smell of dried sweat and public transport.

The following morning there were sightings shared all over the internet of one of the victims – Jayan Ratnam – outside without his skin, crimson flesh against brick wall. He was in front of a Starbucks when the microphones caught up with him, pushed into his face.

'What kind of statement are you making here Jay-an?' they called. 'What do you want the thieves to know?'

He looked terrified, coffee cup in hand, weak sun dappling his face. 'I just had to get to work, I'm not making a statement. But whoever has my skin, give it back.'

They looked disappointed.

* * *

Mariah's skin began to pucker and pale, making a sound like rustling leaves when she rubbed her fingers across it. Concerned this would cause irreparable damage, she started shedding again, folding her skin carefully into the gel at night. She bought an extra lock for her submersion trunk.

Soon after that, it was stolen. Mariah woke to find the front door wide open and an empty spot where her trunk should have been, everything else untouched. The trunk was large, inlaid with pearlescent triangles that repeated in star patterns across its surface. Emma had convinced her to keep it in the living room where they could admire it. But as Mariah stared at that spot – darker where the heavy load used to be – she couldn't help wondering if Emma's real rationale was to keep her own skin safer at the foot of their bed. After all, there were rumours that skin like hers was the primary target. Arms crossed in front of her, Mariah rubbed one thumb across the underside of her arm, bereft at the feeling of the wet muscle instead of that smooth patch of skin she would sometimes stroke in times of distress.

Mariah struggled to sleep, worrying how her skin was being used. Perhaps it was being turned into a bag, or a jumpsuit, like animal skin. She imagined what it would feel like, dried and beaten, polished to a matte finish. She spent days trawling the internet, trying to find a glimpse of it. She would know it if she saw it.

Pacing the flat, she touched things anew: lifting the egg-shaped paperweight her father had brought from a trip back home, the glossy jade smudged by the tacky residue she now left behind; the carpet underfoot transferring tufts of fluff to her soles. She and her home imprinted on each other in this new, sticky body of hers.

She kept the windows shut, broad sunbeams magnified through the glass panes. Eventually the flat started to smell, first of bleach from the thrice daily cleans Emma administered, and then from an odour Mariah couldn't quite place at first, meaty and metallic. Her body was rotting; souring slowly, muscles beginning to grey and separate into a fibrous mass.

Mariah was relieved when Emma left: her skin, the tiny pink scales she scattered around the flat which would sometimes deposit onto Mariah, had begun to feel like a taunt. The flat was too warm for two bodies anyway.

* * *

The acrid smell of her body was becoming too much to bear in that small space, so Mariah began to leave the flat, first to the newsagent downstairs, then further afield to the park, and then she started going out in the evenings with Jayan and Aliya and the others, their numbers having grown to about thirty-five in her little corner of the city. They shared tips on dying their gauze wraps to match the colour of their lost skin (her recipe for a mix of turmeric and coriander powder had turned her limbs a murky green when she unwrapped herself at night), and they wore these outside, underneath long garments. As the night progressed and their gel-soaked gauze began to dry, they took on oddly angular shapes, like cubist portraits come to life.

One Friday night they went out in the north part of the city, dark and wiry trees framing delicate porticos along the street. They moved together, huddled close, so their shadows cast monstrous shapes along pavements slicked wet and pockmarked with grey and pink globs of gum, like it had rained flesh.

The bar was fitted with cherry wood edged in gold, bulbous lamps and palm fronds like some old colonial haunt. Jayan assured them that the band would be good, so they settled into the cluster of maroon leather armchairs and glared back at the rest of the room.

In the crowd along the bar, Mariah saw a spill of blonde hair, almost auburn in the amber light. Untangling herself from the group, she approached, grazing the soft skin with her jagged fingertips. The woman pulled away, grimacing, her small white teeth buried in a large mouth. She smelled familiar. 'Do we know each other?' Mariah asked.

'No, I don't think so.' Sneering, she pulled her hair over one shoulder. Nestled under her left ear was a small beige mark against dark skin, the shape of a teardrop. Mariah struggled to take a breath, and reached out to pinch its raised surface.

'Don't touch me!' the woman screeched. Eyes swivelled in their direction, a collective bated breath, as a tussle ensued. They found themselves ejected from the bar onto the rain-soaked streets, one clutching frantically at the other.

'This isn't yours! I bought it online.'

Mariah paused, panting. 'You bought it, just as it is?'

The woman looked uncomfortable. 'Look,' she said, quieter this time. 'You just need to do some digging and you can find all sorts of things online. You don't have to keep wearing this.' She gestured at Mariah's crusty limbs.

'But the skin you're wearing is *mine*. I've had it my whole life, it's a part of me.'

The woman shrugged, uninterested, and pushed her way back into the bar, leaving Mariah on the pavement outside, tears wetting her gauze.

* * *

Mariah returned to isolating herself in her flat. It was full of trinkets that once belonged to her father: a tiny silver box with a creaky hinge for his baby teeth, darker where the engravings ran deeper;

a framed photograph of him and his brothers, long-limbed with skinny trouser legs rolled up past the ankles, piercings studding the various folds of their faces. Their skin looked like hers. Or what used to be hers. She gripped the frame's thick gold corners, the cool metal giving momentary relief to her warm flesh.

Outside, a story broke about skin swapping, and it made its way back into her flat in fragments.

'We've been doing it for years!' identical twins on the television chimed. 'But does that count as swapping if they look exactly the same either way?' pundits chuckled nervously on Sunday morning programmes. And then there was Ashanti and Joe, the couple who were on all the late-night talk shows and swapped regularly. 'We had to make an agreement to swap every week. It was the only fair thing to do.'

Caught on camera and doing the rounds online was an altercation on a train platform, dimly lit and covered with knobbly mounds of grey slush from the previous day's snowstorm. A lone figure fended off a snarling mob by shedding in front of them and gesturing at his face. They seemed reassured and backed off. Alone again, he slowly pulled his skin back on.

Politicians were interviewed, red-faced and flustered. 'Well of course, with the appropriate legislation we will be able to manage the situation. It's unprecedented, but we need to have some way of identifying people. We need to know people are who they say they are.'

* * *

Mariah poured over pages of listings for weeks, comparing elasticity, colour, and finish, and held glossy photos of her old self to the bright screen to find as close a match to her own skin as possible. She decided on one that should have been more expensive given its lighter tone, but scarring on the shoulders, inner thighs and ankles meant she could afford it.

While she much preferred wearing her new skin to the gauze, she found herself itching constantly. At night, she would scrape her nails along the softest parts until they became red and coarse, and sometimes bright pinpricks of blood would appear. The scratching continued until her whole body stung and she had to shed earlier than planned, dispensing the skin into her new submersion trunk.

Over the course of several weeks' incessant scratching, small holes started to appear in the skin, slowly growing to larger gashes, until eventually when she put it into her submersion trunk it began to shred and fray. Realising she could not salvage it, she took a perverse pleasure in seeing it disintegrate, subsumed in the gluey interior.

'This is what I get for buying cheap,' she thought to herself.

In their group chat, Jayan and Aliya sent her links for more reputable online skin sellers. 'M, this one is better, they give a certificate of proof that it's not stolen.'

'Also check this one, locally sourced only.'

The thought of having to go through the process all over again filled Mariah with dread. Instead, the next morning she pulled herself out of bed and began wrapping herself carefully with gauze, gently weaving it in and out between her limbs. She tucked the loose ends into folds and threaded earrings into the fabric where her ears were.

Her friends protested. 'You're only hurting yourself, you know. Do we even know how long you can survive without skin?'

She stopped responding and was eventually removed from the group chat.

* * *

Mariah walked through the office, her third job in as many months, with its shiny windows and computer screens. People stared, gleaming cheekbones and supple necks turned towards her, first quizzically, then with disgust. She increased her pace, keen to get to the basement.

Once down there she was relieved for the company of silence. The air was thick with dust swirling slowly across the room, never quite settling on any of the surfaces. Neat horizontal lines cut across the walls: shelves crowded with books and magazines and long-forgotten pamphlets.

At the centre of the room was Mariah's table, surrounded by office chairs without armrests or backs, and metal poles jutting menacingly from their centre. Her chair was mostly intact, just a little askew from a missing wheel. Next to her were two stacks of yellowing papers. She inhaled deeply each time she moved a sheet from one pile to the other as the smell of mildew and old resin became dislodged. Entering each page's archival digits in her spreadsheet, her fingers – swollen with fabric – would crackle and scrape each time they landed on the keyboard in a raspy melody.

In the lethargy of her day, she would let her mind wander to Jayan and Aliya and the others in their new skins, and the little community they had created together, without her.

And then she would continue on her keyboard, crunching away.

MISS JUNIPER'S ACADEMY FOR WILD GIRLS

Jen Campbell

Miss Juniper clapped her hands for quiet. 'Girls! It is almost time for our Christmas dance.'

Everyone quivered. It was the season of spiced foods, dried flowers and soft slippers. Many of the girls wrote home for treats. For food, for dresses – for gloves. Those who received replies were sent treasures in boxes of cherry wood, hurried in through the oak doors to stop the snow scurrying in behind. Even so, Sister Elizabeth often complained that the hallway was covered in sludge.

'You will turn our home into an ice rink!' she snapped, slipping on the tiles, and far from having the desired effect of stopping us traipsing rain-soaked through the hall, Abigail tried to work out just how much water we would need, and at what temperature, to turn the whole downstairs into an ice palace.

The classrooms were cold during the day. They said it was good for us, but I didn't believe it. As we decorated the walls for winter, Miriam told Miss Juniper that we should invest in lamps made of soapstone, and that, instead of burning oil in the evenings, we should burn seal fat like those who live in the Arctic.

'My father knows all about it,' she boasted. 'He's travelled as far north as you can go. At home, we've a narwhal tusk on our mantelpiece. Pa even bested a polar bear in a game of Whist.'

'Bears don't play cards,' snorted Abigail.

Miriam stuck out her chin defiantly. 'And how would you know? You've gone no further north than Scotland.'

Abigail scowled, stabbing cloves into the belly of a tangerine.

Outside, our world turned blue.

'This year, we're having a bal masqué,' Miss Juniper said, as we buzzed around her at lunchtime. 'You shall each dress up as an animal. Think of the costumes you will create, girls! Think of the invisibility!'

Her cheeks flushed as she touched each of our noses in turn. 'Think of what you will wear – how you will cover your skin,' and she winked at me then, before extending her arms to the group. 'Think of the freedom!'

Harriet nudged me, bouncing in her kitten heels. 'They've done this for you, Amber, can't you see?'

I could – and I hated them for it.

December brewed. As the night sky gathered its skirts, we chose our animals.

Miriam wrote home to ask her father what clothes a polar bear might wear to a party.

Abigail asked if she could camp out in the woods to study bad-tempered badgers.

Harriet stole all the peacock feathers from Mei's prized dressing gown and was made to eat bread and marmalade for a week.

I wanted to hibernate.

We were a zoo.

At night-time, our dorm was a mess of animal noises. Sophie crowed when the sun rose – she called it method acting – and Tamsin walked around on all fours for two days, before putting holes in her best tights and admitting a graceful defeat.

I did not know what I should be.

I thought of blue whales and their songs that no one could interpret. I thought of a platypus, our real-life chimera, put together piece by piece. Part of me longed to be a dragon, just to see the looks on their faces: me, the girl who dared to breathe fire, even after all that, but then a notice went up above the tuck box saying: *'All costumes must be true to life. No unicorns. No mermaids. No exceptions.'*

Heaven forbid we should be exceptional women.

On the way to church on Sunday, we peered in at the dark windows of *Mr Collins's Establishment*. We couldn't spy the boys, although Miriam swore she saw a cluster of shadows hiding in a corner.

'All boys are made of shadows,' she breathed, as we bowed our heads in prayer. 'You should never walk beside one when the sun is setting for that reason.'

Abigail looked unconvinced.

'I'm serious,' she hissed. 'At that time of day, their shadows are long enough to swallow a girl whole.'

We all thought of Rosaleen. We opened our hymn sheets and cleared our frog throats. As we sang of winter kings, we pictured rows of boys with mouths like caves.

I decided I would be a fox three days before the dance. An Arctic fox for ease, for we had no orange paint, and while the others helped Sister Elizabeth cut snowflakes from newspapers, I crept into the attic and picked at the cream wallpaper. I peeled it off in sheets, glued these feathered strips to my cardboard mask, and pierced holes for eyes. Later, I would make myself a dress from a long-sleeved leotard and a bedsheet but, in that moment, I did the foxtrot in my culottes and admired my paper mask in a dusty mirror.

I curtseyed, my bare arms glistening different colours in the scattered light.

'You look like a jigsaw,' Miriam had said to me once, running a hand along my arm without actually touching it. 'Or a snake that's shed its skin and fallen asleep half-way through.' She'd smiled as though this were a compliment. 'I'm sure my father would love to study you.'

She'd waited for me to respond but my words had run away from me. I always think of what to say when it's too late to say it. Instead, as Miriam stared at me, my words sat in a corner of my brain and talked amongst themselves. Embarrassed and unsure how to dress.

Abigail was told she wasn't allowed to camp in the forest, even in the name of researching badgers so, grudgingly, she spent her time reading books instead. Our library was not as grand as some but it was the smallest room, which meant it was always warm. I took to joining her, the two of us creeping down the stone steps at midnight like miniature ghosts.

We studied nocturnal creatures – gripping quills, underlining facts.

The word *shenanigan* is derived from the Irish expression *sionnachuighim,* meaning 'I play the fox.'

The fox is one of the most sacred animals of the goddess Ninhursag.

In Chinese mythology there's a fox with nine tails.

In Japan, a fox-human is called a kitsune.

A group of foxes is known as an earth.

Foxes can see the earth's magnetic field, and they use this to hunt.

'And look at this,' Abigail said, waving a book under my nose that smelled faintly of vanilla. 'Foxes were often burned along with women suspected of witchcraft. People thought they were the Devil.' She giggled to herself, turning the page. 'Says nothing in here about badgers, though.'

Abigail didn't tiptoe around me. She didn't think to apologise for talking about burning women. I sank back into my battered armchair and listened happily to her reciting a song from the south of France about a wolf, a fox and a hare dancing around a tree.

On the day of the dance, the academy was in chaos. Five fir trees were dragged into the parlour, each decorated with brightly wrapped sweets. Miss Juniper had been awake since sunrise, baking twenty fruit pies. Sister Elizabeth hurried from room to room, blessing all the furniture. Every so often she looked anxiously out of the window, peering down the cobbled streets, as though expecting to find mischief there.

But the mischief was upstairs.

Our dorm was the backstage of a carnival. The half-stage of a metamorphosis. Trunks were flung open, their innards strewn everywhere. Miriam had smuggled in a bottle of port, which we downed like pirates, first pretending to like it, then pretending to be drunk in a way that was infectious.

Thus, our costuming began.

Sophie bravely disembowelled a pillow, sticking its feathers to her face.

Harriet dyed her legs with tea leaves, drawing a line up the back with charcoal to give the illusion of stockings.

'Do peacocks wear stockings?'

Abigail had raided Miss Juniper's stationery cupboard. She sat cross-legged in front of the mirror, dragging white chalk across her cheeks to mark out badger stripes against her dark skin.

'Do I look fierce yet?' she snarled, baring her teeth.

I tottered, half-in, half-out of my long white dress.

'Deadly,' I grinned, and pulled on my mask.

We emerged:
a polar bear
a peacock
a silkie chicken
an Arctic fox
a badger
a butterfly
a deer.

We inched towards the banister as the cold air raced in. There were mumbled voices down below, the awkward laugh of Miss Juniper taking coats, and Sister Elizabeth telling Mr Collins not to worry in the slightest about his boys' snowy feet.

'We've not gone to any trouble,' she lied smoothly. 'Come on through!'

Miriam had researched boys the same way I'd researched foxes. She said they were vampiric. That some had lost their mirror reflections. She said to make sure they didn't whistle through their teeth.

'Whistling invites demons,' she said, throwing a dark look at Sophie, who often sang in the shower. 'Best of luck, ladies!' Here, her voice gave a wobble. 'Should one of you be chosen, you must remember to write.'

We paraded down the staircase, trying not to trip over our lop-sided costumes. The long sleeves of my leotard were itchy, the seams catching on my skin, but I pointed my toes and stood tall, just like Miss Juniper had taught us.

There we were: a party of girls. Collective nouns had always enthralled me –

a smack of jellyfish

a parliament of owls

a cauldron of bats

a prickle of porcupines.

The boys were lined up in the parlour. A troop, a tower, a shadow. They were dressed in velvet suits. Their costumes simple eye masks so they were easy to identify. I squinted at them, looking for signs of Rosaleen. There was only one new boy. He wore a suit of deep maroon, there was a patch of hair on his neck that he'd missed when shaving, and he was eying Miriam's polar bear costume with something like a smirk.

'Welcome, all,' Miss Juniper beamed. 'Mr Collins, I'd like to thank you for taking the time to come and examine our collection of girls.'

He raised a glass of sherry and she blushed furiously.

'I hope your gentlemen like what they see.'

She turned on the gramophone, and the games began.

First, there was Pin the Tail on the Donkey. Some of the boys had brought needles from home. Extra sharp, for extra fun. The game ended unfortunately, with a pin stuck in the back of Mei's leg.

Next: Squeak Piggy Squeak. The tallest became the farmer. Blindfolded with black ribbon, he sat on each of our laps in turn, using his hands to guess who we were. He didn't know our names, so instead he guessed our animals. Miriam's costume was covered in cotton wool, so it was obvious who she was, but when he sat on her lap, he pretended not to know, so he could touch her for longer.

And so it went.

Since the fire, we had not played Snapdragon – a game where you eat raisins covered in brandy as they're set alight – so, instead, we played Wink Murder, Deerstalker, Cupid's Coming. I did my best to play my part, to duck my head, to peer out through my paper mask: a fox cub in the night. It was a vicious conflict. Being chosen by the boys was the only way to leave. But who on earth knew where they would drag us? Our letters to Rosaleen always came back, unopened.

I kept my eyes locked on Abigail. She stuck out her tongue whenever she caught me looking.

'Is it true, Miss Fox?'

I jumped. The newest boy hovered by my ear.

'If you see a bear, you should not run,' Abigail had said to me on one of our library nights, reading from a book on hunting. 'You should avoid eye contact and slowly walk away. But! If a bear approaches you, Amber, you should stand your ground – for you cannot outrun it.'

I stood my ground.

'Is what true?' I smiled sweetly, although my mask covered most of my face.

'Is it true that you're hiding a monster?' He gave a guffaw – the laughter of someone sensing a trap. He gazed around the room, looking at each of us in turn. 'The boys tell me one of you is half-burned to a crisp, though I rather think they're having me on.'

The floor became a swamp.

'What say you?' His breath smelled of mud. 'Which one of you is cooked?'

The doors to the parlour opened and Sister Elizabeth appeared pushing two trolleys heavy with food. The boys descended. Bruised fruit and pastry crumbs. Red stains on the tablecloth.

In the far corner of the room, beneath a bouquet of mistletoe, Mr Collins handed Miss Juniper a leather bag filled with gold. Enough to keep our academy open for one more year. All for the gift of a girl.

Miriam's voice cut through the hum. 'Actually, my father says polar bears are very intelligent.'

'Your father?' The tallest boy leered. 'I thought none of you had any family. I thought that was why you were here.'

Miriam's cheeks flushed pink. 'My father loves me very much.'

'No need to show off,' Mei hobbled back into the room, her butterfly wings forlorn, her leg crisscrossed with a bandage.

'Some of us still have family,' Abigail shrugged. 'They just don't want us to come home.'

'Why's that?'

Sophie batted her eyelids ironically. 'We're too wild for them.'

The boys howled, clinking their glasses. The tallest started to whistle the melody of *Come Upstairs, My Darling*, and I saw Miriam's eyes flicker towards the cake knife.

a shiver of sharks

a cackle of hyenas

a murder of crows

'It's time for dancing!'

Miss Juniper and Mr Collins rolled back the rug, exposing the naked floor. The boys threw their napkins into the fire, prowling beneath the chandelier. They looked hungrily from girl to girl. Sister Elizabeth never stayed for this part. She made her usual excuses and retired to her room, with an apricot scone and a sigh.

'I want the polar bear,' the tallest boy drawled.

'I'll take the broken butterfly.'

'The peacock!'

Soon there was a mess of limbs and feathers. The two-step, the polka, the mazurka. Shadows stretching like trees. I backed up against the patterned wallpaper, sheltered by the grandfather clock.

'Care to join, Miss Fox?' the newest boy held out his blueberry-stained palm.

I stared at it numbly.

Behind him, Miriam was dancing violently, baring her teeth as though she would rip someone's throat.

My words finally emerged from their corners. 'It's me,' I said.

He raised his voice above the music. 'What's you?'

'Me,' I repeated, firmly. 'I'm the one who was burned.'

His grin faltered. 'You're messing with me, too.'

Sophie leapt onto a table.

He prodded me with a finger. 'Prove it.'

I imagined pulling off my leotard and exposing my arms. The quilting of skin grafts. The shining of scar tissue.

'No.'

He pulled roughly at my sleeve. 'Go on.'

'I said, no!' I shoved him hard, and he fell back into the pile of dancers. He shouted vile names. Caves of noise. The other boys jeered and pulled him up, dragging him into a ferocious waltz.

an unkindness of ravens

a bellowing of bullfinches

a cloud of gnats

'Psst!' I turned to see a finger beckoning wildly through the door. I grabbed Abigail's hand and she pulled me into the unlit hall. As the door shut behind us, the menace of the party descended into grunts and muffled bellows, all slightly off-key.

We stood still for several minutes, our meat-hearts pounding, our backs against the varnished wood. A couplet.

I peeled my mask from my face.

It was much colder in the hall. The floor was still covered in the boys' snowy footprints. They'd frozen in the dark to form a brittle, crisp pond.

'You know,' said Abigail. 'I found one more fox story.'

I smiled at her, her badger stripes glistening.

'People in Finland used to say foxes made the Northern Lights.'

She rested her head on my shoulder.

'They used to say foxes ran across the snow. That they sent sparks from their tails into the night-time sky.'

We closed our eyes, imagining the colours.

There was a crash and a roar from the universe behind us. A toppling of tables. A smashing of plates.

We began to tiptoe across the frozen pond, hoping the world would not crack beneath us.

We took one step, then another.

I did not let go of her hand.

SINKH♡LE

Emma Hutton

Dear Suzy,
Your heart is a sinkh♡le.
Love, You-Know-Who.

Every week You-Know-Who ordered '*Suspiria*-red' roses for Suzy. The time they said to replace the 'o' in sinkhole with a heart, I nearly lost my mind. I couldn't get over it. All that passion. I wished I was Suzy, but I'm not. I'm Zola. I work at Flower Power, a floral concept store. It's not just flowers, we sell candles, and soap, and bags made out of old tyres. The owner is my best friend, Jules. That's how I got the gig. We've known each other since we were kids. We used to share baths when we were wee and cigarettes when we got older. We live together now. Jules thinks I live in a fantasy world. She says I watch too many romance films but it's her that's always covered in a blanket on the sofa watching *The Philadelphia Story*. I work behind the till and write all the cards at Flower Power. The cards are always about babies and baptisms and brides and dead bodies. And they're always from people who are sorry, or thankful or somewhere over the moon. People are so predictable.

I used to be a primary school teacher, but I lost my job after I bit one of the children. I said it then and I'll say it again: Don't put your finger in my mouth if you don't want me to bite it. I was always a biter. My mother said it started from day one and if I'd been born with teeth I would have 'had her tits off.' She used to say it was her fault because they had to cut me out of her. 'You got the taste for blood,' she would say, tucking me in.

Before I could walk, I tried to bite the dog and then the cat. But it wasn't until my teeth came in that I started to realise the damage I could do. Paresh Shah had to get his lip stitched back on. Bella Doone will forevermore have a full moon of teeth marks on her left shoulder. Sammy Maxwell lost a chunk out of his arm. I only wanted them to love me, but nobody wants a biter. I have to warn the people I'm with. Some listen better than others. They always like it at first, teeth on skin. But that soon fades.

Dear Suzy,
I'd like to see you at the bottom of the sea.
Love, You-Know-Who.

'Zola, have you thought that this You-Know-Who might actually be a psychopath? Like, a proper murdery psychopath.' Jules is sat on the living room floor cutting up old Christmas cards so she can turn them into new Christmas cards. She likes to make new things out of old things. She's so thrifty.

'He's not a psycho. He's passionate.'

'How do you even know it's a he?'

'I just do. I have a feeling and that feeling is that he might be the right person for me.'

'Okay well he said her heart is a sinkhole. What does that even mean? Is your heart a sinkhole?'

'I wish my heart was a sinkhole. A big, beautiful sinkhole that grows and grows and pulls everything into it. Like the ones on TV that suck in trees and cars and babies in buggies. If my heart was a sinkhole I could suck You-Know-Who right in.'

Jules hums. She's not convinced about my obsession with You-Know-Who. She likes to say she enjoys the idea of love, but she understands the reality of it. She's been seeing The Doctor for almost a year but refuses to call her that. Instead she says The Doctor is 'my little friend' like she's Al Pacino in *Scarface*. The first night they fucked she asked The Doctor to check her moles. Jules is very pragmatic and the smartest person I know. She wears a locket with a picture of herself inside. The picture is her as a six-year-old in overalls and white star shaped sunglasses. It reminds her to give herself a break, to be kind to the little her. See – she's so smart! To be fair, it's the oldest trick in the therapist's book: *Would you be this hard on the little you?* Jules sucks on the locket when she thinks, which is a lot. I worry about her perfect teeth. The Doctor, Jules' girlfriend, thinks she should put a picture of her in the locket. She even gave her a passport photo to put in it. Ugh. I try not to hate The Doctor.

I've been to all kinds of therapists since biting Paresh's lip off in the playground. I even went away on a 'retreat' for a little while. I've sucked on endless lollies and spat out enough gum to cover as much sky as I can see. I tried biting myself but it wasn't the same. My last therapist told me my biting is a confused kind of intimacy and I should 'find my kind.' I looked online and it turns out 'my kind' is the kind that wants to do more than just bite.

The last real relationship I had was with the Substitute Teacher. He said Edith Wharton was his favourite writer, but he'd never even heard of *Ethan Frome*. He wrote me rhyming poems about roller coasters and spiders. He rhymed love with glove and dove. I was allowed to suck on his underarm but one time I went for his neck and he pushed me off the sofa. 'No neck,' he said and wagged his finger. After the biting incident with the child he said I couldn't be trusted and I was secretly grateful to Clementine Ridley and her desire to stick fingers in open holes. We had one last night together and in the morning I bit all the rubber buttons off his remote controls and spat them out the window.

I got 'back out there' pretty quickly because that's what I was supposed to do. Jules told me I should bide my time, but love waits for no woman. I met Salami Man on a dating app. He was my only match. I'd decided to go with honesty as the best policy. My bio read: *I don't like to fight, I like to bite.* Everyone's always telling each other to be themselves. So, I was trying to be myself. I wanted someone to sink my teeth into. We went for drinks and after he asked if we could stop off at a corner shop. We did and he bought a pack of salami. He ate the whole thing himself with his hands and didn't offer me any. In bed, I bit his lip and his wrist but then he said, 'that's enough.'

'What about my bio?' I asked as he put his salami-smelling hand over my mouth. While he slept, I got dressed and closed the windows before taking a little chunk out of his backside. I knew he'd be a screamer.

Dear Suzy,
I hope you get fucked by a bear.
Love, You-Know-Who.

Turns out You-Know-Who owns a paint shop. I know this because I found his name on the order system and then I googled him. Up popped Splatter, a fancy paint shop he owned. There was a picture of him inside a drawing of a paint tin. He had a beard and he looked quite tired. I also found some pictures of him with a woman with dark hair cut into a square. In most of the photos she is wearing red lipstick and clinging onto him with one hand and making a fist with the other. I wondered if she was Suzy with the sinkhole heart. She looked like a Suzy.

Splatter doesn't smell like paint. It smells like rat traps and the antiseptic wipes you rub across children's scraped knees. It's not as fancy as it looks on the website.

'I can't believe you dragged me out of bed on a Saturday for this. This is legit stalker territory. You're Meg-Ryan-in-Sleepless-in-Seattle levels of bananas right now.' Jules is sucking her locket. 'We should not be here.'

'Shhh. Don't you want me to find *my kind*, Jules?'

Jules rolls her eyes, picks up a card full of yellow squares and fans her face with it. 'My little friend wants you to stop biting me.'

The Doctor. I hate The *fucking* Doctor with her stupid shiny hair and how she always takes my space on the sofa. She's always lining up tins in the kitchen cupboard and sighing when I walk into a room. I heard them arguing last night. About flowers. Jules wants The Doctor to buy her flowers but The Doctor doesn't get it. 'Why on earth why would I buy you flowers when you own a florist?' I pressed my ear against the wall and willed Jules to explode but she just quietly said, 'Because I love flowers.' The Doctor could have pulled weeds out of a wall and stuck them in a jam jar and Jules would have screamed with delight. But if she really loved her she would have got her carnations, Jules' absolute favourite. She thinks they got a bad rep for being boring because of that time Charlotte from *Sex and the City* called them 'filler flowers.' We couldn't watch it after that and she started putting way too many carnations into almost every bunch she made. 'I just want them to be loved,' she'd say, slipping the stems in. Ugh. I hate The Doctor.

I pick up a card covered in white squares and stare intently at one called Stone White. I don't really bite Jules. Not anymore. Not since we were teenagers. I suck. Mostly the inside of her elbow when we're watching murder shows. Occasionally she gives me her ankle. Sometimes I forget myself and nip a little. Sometimes I think she lets me forget myself. She used to ask if she could bite me back but I always said no, I didn't want her to get the taste for it and end up like me. She doesn't ask any more.

'She found teeth marks on the last mole inspection.'

But I was so careful, I wonder if Jules is lying.

A man appears next to me gesturing at the card full of white squares that I'm now waving in front of my face. 'Looking for something in white?' It's You-Know-Who with his beard wearing a plaid shirt and jeans. He smiles and I look at his wrists and then at his mouth. I feel sick. Sick in a good way. He looks like a detective that never gives up. The one that will find your dead daughter or die trying.

'Do you have white? Not this Stone White or Caspar White. Just white-white.'

'What about Stalker White?' Jules whispers.

'We can do white-white,' he smiles. 'A matte finish?'

I nod.

'One tin?'

I nod.

'OK, let me get that for you,' he says, walking off. 'See you up at the till.'

'He smells weird. Like that blue ice cream we used to eat when we were kids. I don't like it.'

'Jules, don't.'

'Zola and the weird guy sitting in a tree…'

Jules doesn't like anyone I like. She never has. Maybe he does smell a bit weird but so what. Everyone smells weird now. It's all wet concrete, a rose in Chernobyl, trapped sunlight in an undiscovered monk's cave. The last perfume I bought, the woman at the counter described it as: 'Imagine you've escaped from the witch's oven in Hansel and Gretel. You are running. You are finally free.' It smells like burning hair, gingerbread and trees.

I leave Jules with the yellows and head for the reds.

'Red?' He appears out of nowhere. Conjured. 'It's a tricky colour,' he says, looking at the card full of red squares in my hand. 'People are afraid of it. Most use it as a feature wall in the kitchen or for a kid's playroom. Are you afraid of it?'

'I'm not afraid of red,' I say and point to one I think looks like the colour of my insides split open. Red roses. Almost neon. 'This one reminds me of something.'

He leans over for a closer look. 'That's Red Stallion 2. My favourite. Would you like a tester?'

'*Suspiria*.'

'Excuse me?'

'It reminds me of the colour of the blood in *Suspiria*. The film.' I look at him and wait for something to happen. He closes his eyes for a second and I imagine what's behind them: the breaking apart of a stained-glass ceiling, the sway of a body like a metronome, arterial-red blood dripping onto a checkerboard floor.

He opens his eyes. 'That's my favourite film.'

'Mine too,' I lie. 'I love all the blood.'

He tilts his hips towards me and I look for a wall to press my back into.

'The original, obviously.'

'Obviously,' I nod and tongue my cheek, frilled and white from biting at my own self.

He plucks the card full of red out of my hand. 'Do you want to go for dinner with me?'

'I do,' I say and I smile with all of my teeth.

On Tuesday a woman with a square haircut comes into the shop. She's got a fistful of red roses. Jules has gone to pick up lunch so it's just me. Me and Suzy. Me and Suzy in the shop. She pushes a card across the counter. It's the one I wrote last week. I pick it up.

Dear Suzy,
I dreamt you were dead and it was wonderful.
Love, You-Know-Who.

My handwriting really is beautiful. We don't value penmanship enough these days. Fucking computers. You can see where the nib has touched the card, the rise of fall of the ink linking everything together like stars in a constellation. A perfect tumult flowing like champagne from a mountain of George Best glasses. A tamed Twombly.

'Excuse me.' The woman's face has turned as red as the flowers.

'How can I help?' I act cheerier than usual.

'I need you to stop sending me these flowers.'

'Oh. Is there something wrong with them?'

'It's not the flowers, it's the man who sends them. It's my ex. He sends those horrible cards.' She points at the card in my hand.

'Oh, I'm sorry. We thought it might be a lovers' in-joke.'

'It's not a joke.' She starts shaking the flowers in her tight little fist. 'He's insane.'

'Insane?' Potato, potahto.

'He rowed us out to a tiny island in the middle of a lake and left me there. He said if I loved him as much as he loved me I would find my way across the water back to him. There were swans.'

I think I like You-Know-Who even more. I want to tell Suzy that true love isn't meant to be easy, that it's a battlefield. It's a test. But I don't say anything because she clearly does not understand love or romance. Poor Suzy, doesn't she know you've got to fight for a love that's real?

'I was out there all night. Waiting for someone to find me.'

'Can't you swim?'

'It was November.'

'So, you really didn't love him?'

Her mouth opens and I want to lean across and shut it before drool comes out. 'If you don't stop sending these fucking flowers I will go to the police.'

She launches the flowers across the counter and storms out the door just as Jules walks in. 'Suzy with the sinkhole heart?'

'That's the one.'

Jules flips the sign on the door and locks it. 'What did she say?'

I tell her about the boat and the lake and watch as Jules' eyes get bigger.

'OK, there's no way you are going out with that creep tonight. No way. You hear me?'

I tut. Jules hates my taste. 'Suzy's exaggerating and that's her loss. He was trying to prove how much he loved her.'

'That's your takeaway from her story? That he loved her? Jesus Christ, Zola.'

'Don't worry about it. You met him. He was fine.'

'I saw him for one minute and he didn't seem like anything. Please don't go tonight. I'll ditch my date with The Doctor and we can stay in. We can watch *You've Got Mail.*'

'I need to find my own Doctor, Jules. Don't you want that for me?'

'If he ends up murdering you it's your own fault.' She drops a cheese sandwich on the counter for me and walks out to the back, kicking a bucket of dahlias as she goes.

'You've got tiny little teeth. Perfect little squares.' You-Know-Who reaches out but doesn't touch my face.

'Thank you, I'm a grinder.'

'What do you do?'

'I work at Flower Power. It's my best friend's shop.' He doesn't flinch. 'It's a floral concept store.'

The waiter comes and tells us the specials in a sonorously deep Italian accent that might be fake. You-Know-Who says he wants the seafood pasta and I should have it too. I nod and feel my phone vibrate in my pocket. I know it's Jules because it's always Jules and I'm sure it's going to be her saying sorry for freaking out and making sure I'm alive. I pull it out onto the table and You-Know-

Who clears his throat.

Bring booze back. The Doctor's dead to me.

'Oh shit.'

'Is everything okay?'

But then the food comes and I don't know if everything is okay. The spaghetti is full of mussels that look like sun-wasted buoys and slippy squid rings that I swallow down whole. He cuts his spaghetti with a knife and fork. I wind the strands around my fork and look at him, smiling. We don't speak for a very long time and I wonder if this is a test I might be passing. Eventually the waiter clears our plates and pours out another glass of wine from the bottle of white You-Know-Who chose without looking at the list.

'I don't like to talk during dinner. I think it's a sacred time, don't you?'

I start to wonder what I think but before I can get anywhere all the waiters in their white shirts are singing and one approaches our table holding two tiny plates. On each sits a square of chocolate cake with a shiny pink rose.

You-Know-Who leans over, 'Smile and play along. When I booked, I told them it was your birthday. You get free cake for birthdays. Buon compleanno!'

'My birthday's not until June,' I say when the waiters leave.

'Don't you want your cake?'

'I don't like cake.'

'But I got it for you. You should eat it. Go on,' he says, pushing the little plate towards me. 'Do it for me.'

Cake reminds me of children's parties that I either ruined or didn't get invited to. 'I'll take it home for my friend.' Chocolate is Jules' favourite but she's not that picky.

You-Know-Who scowls when I ask the waiter to wrap it up for me. His face turns red when the cake is brought back to me parcelled in a tin foil swan and I remember the red-faced woman in the flower shop.

'I didn't order cake for your friend, I ordered it for you. If you don't want it, I'll take it back.' He reaches for the swan's neck but I bat his hand away. At first I think he's playing. But then he does it again and again, eventually we're both standing up and he's trying to wrestle the swan away from me.

'That cake is for Jules!'

The next time he lifts his hand, I grab it and put it to my mouth. I bite the soft fleshy bit between the thumb and forefinger. It's a good bit. I get carried away and tear a little. When he starts to howl I let go and make a run for it, out the door and down the dark street. I flag down the bus that's almost pulling away; the silver swan must have got the driver's attention. 'Thanks for stopping,' I pant and smile.

'You've got something in your teeth, love.'

I don't go straight home, or to the newsagent to buy cheap red wine and the jelly dinosaurs Jules likes to bite the arms off of. I end up at Flower Power, on my hands and knees pulling carnations out of all the bunches on the floor set up for delivery tomorrow and I start laughing because there are hundreds of them. All different colours. I dump the stems out one by one until it looks like a weird pyre in the middle of the shop floor. There are way too many to carry. I gather up as many as I can, put them on the counter and wrap them up in brown paper. When I reach for the heaviest white note card I hear Jules in my ear, in her best Katharine Hepburn voice, 'Ooooh fancy.' But then there's a key in the door and she's stood there in a dressing gown over pyjamas, hair half up, half down, sandals with socks underneath.

'Zola, what the fuck?' She's looking at what's left of the floral pyre.

'Are those my pyjamas?'

'I got a call saying the alarm went off.'

'It did but I reset it.'

'Zola, what's going on? Did something happen?'

'I was going to bring you some filler flowers home,' I gesture to the bunch on the counter and the debris on the floor.

'Nobody wants them, Zola.'

'You do,' I laugh. 'You love them. And I got you cake. It's chocolate,' I say, picking up the silver swan from the counter and holding it out by its battered neck. 'And something did happen.'

'Z, you're freaking me out,' she says, dodging carnations to grab the silver neck.

'I figured it out when I was biting You-Know-Who.'

'He let you bite him?'

'Not exactly. Hang on,' I say, pulling a pen from the pot.

'What did you figure out?'

I gently press the nib against the card, letting the letter tilt and swerve before lifting it up to my lips and blowing.

'Zola, are you okay?'

'Here.' I hold out the card to her. 'I'll be okay" I say biting my lip as she pulls it from between my fingers and reads.

Dear Jules,
Your heart is a sinkh♡le.
Love, Zola.

'We'll be okay,' I say, watching as she smiles with all her teeth.

TO PEEL AN ORANGE

Beverley Ho

My mother told me to pick out two oranges. Choose the best ones you can find, she said, her eyes avoiding mine, before hurrying off to pick up other supplies. And so, I rummage through the oranges, looking for the biggest, brightest and roundest. I pick them up and press my fingers gently into the skin and weigh them in my hands. I vaguely remember Poh-Poh telling me on one of the rare occasions I accompanied her to the market that the heavier the orange, the juicier. For a moment I pause, the orange in my hand suddenly heavy. Only the best, I think. I lose myself in this process. Then, satisfied with what I have, I pay the man who runs the stall and go to find my mother, the two prized oranges rustling softly in the plastic bag.

* * *

It's half seven when I get out of work, mind mashed to a pulp and a dull ache in my shoulders. My stomach growls in disapproval. As I step out of the cool, air-conditioned building, I'm enveloped by the warm, sticky air, plucked from one extreme climate to the other. It's something I wonder if I'll ever get used to. Outside, a dampened throb of noise and activity greets me. Usually, the streets are alive:

frowning office workers spilling out of glassy skyscrapers at rush hour; people lining in queues outside restaurants, heads bent fervently over phones; the hum of engines and the blare of car horns. Today, the air is somewhat stiller, punctuated by the ticking of the pedestrian crossings, louder than ever before.

I unbutton the top of my blouse, roll up my sleeves and head for the noodle restaurant. A few people are queueing outside, and it doesn't take long before I'm seated at a table with four seats, three of which are already occupied. Having to share tables with strangers has become less uncomfortable, less intrusive. In a city brimming with millions, the boundary I'd like to draw around myself is a luxury I cannot afford. I order my usual and watch as the old man opposite me slurps his noodles, chopsticks moving swiftly between bowl and mouth. The girl next to me reaches over to touch her boyfriend's hand, before leaning in for a kiss. My upper lip curls slightly before I avert my eyes to find something else to look at. The TV mounted on the wall is showing the evening news, clips of large crowds gathering on a main road near the government offices, a swarming sea of indistinguishable heads.

'The protests,' the girl next to me says to her boyfriend in Cantonese sing-song. 'They started tonight. Are you sure we shouldn't join?' He shakes his head and motions for her to hurry up and eat. A waitress throws a bowl of wonton noodles in front of me, soup slopping over the sides onto the table. Service remains as efficient as ever.

I'm out of the restaurant within twenty minutes. When I first moved to Hong Kong, I lingered for a little too long after a meal and the waitress coughed and jutted her chin toward the door. My time here has been characterised by such moments, stumbling and adapting to new social codes. Holding doors open for people is met with suspicious looks and no word of thanks; letting people go in front of you means you get left behind. Navigating this city, a man-eat-man world, is a cut-throat ride. Even the simple things are a persistent jarring reminder: I might look like everyone else, but I am not one of them.

Perhaps, that is why most nights after my jaunt to the noodle shop, I gravitate towards Soho. The glittering district of clubs and bars, frequented by expats as well as locals. Months ago, I arrived, fresh-faced and bright-eyed, in my parents' homeland, embarking on a new adventure. I'll blend in here, I told myself. And I tried. Dancing along to the unrelenting pulse of the city until my feet grew weary and the rhythm moved on without me. So, I end up in Soho, a place of in-between, for a few drinks. Only a few. They steel me against my Poh-Poh's sharp glares when I get home; she's tired of having to live with the inadequate overseas-born, *too-foreign* offspring of her daughter. Someone like Elsie, my typical Hong Kong born-and-bred co-worker, would suit her perfectly.

Tonight, I hesitate for a moment, wondering if I should go home. But I want company that won't moan or nag, so an hour later, I'm in my usual seat by the bar, elbows propped on the wooden surface sticky with spilt alcohol, looking out for another lone soul. Hong Kong is rife with expat men, let loose in a hedonistic playground that proffers easy alcohol, easy drugs, searching for an easy fling as if it were their birth-right. But tonight, they all seem to be taken. I signal to the bartender with my empty glass and he snatches it from my grasp. There's a dull throbbing in my head, a beat out of step with the music blasting from the speakers. It numbs out all traces of disappointed grandmothers and fake, competitive work colleagues.

My refilled glass is dumped in front of me and I take it gladly, the icy reprieve sliding down my throat. I'm about to ask for another when my phone rings. Uncle Albert. Surely Poh-Poh didn't complain to him about our argument last night? I put my phone on silent. I won't have him pestering me now, he has more than enough time to say his piece at family dinners. The screen lights up again – another drink – and again.

I groan and slide off the bar stool. I push through the hordes of people milling around outside and find an alleyway away from the chatter and laughter. Taking a deep breath, I call my uncle.

He answers within a second. 'Cynthia!' I cringe at the way he mutilates my name, how he shapes the 'th' sound into a rough 'f'.

'Uncle Albert,' I reply, careful not to slur my words. I ready myself for a lecture on the importance of filial piety. Did my Western upbringing not teach me anything about respecting elders?

'Your Poh-Poh is in hospital. Where are you?'

The throbbing in my head sharpens. A slight breeze runs through the air. There is only silence. Then, a flurry of questions. Only one finds its way out of my throat.

'What... what happened?'

His voice, softer but still urgent: 'She collapsed. She's still unconscious. The doctors are checking her now. Come quickly. Let me know when you're here – Prince of Wales Hospital, near City One. I'll meet you outside.' I can hear someone on the other end speaking to him. 'I've got to go.'

He hangs up, leaving me clutching my phone to my ear and crumpling against the wall. I try to gather my breath, try to steady my quivering hands. A group of expats swagger by and one of them, wearing a smug look and a shirt that clings too tightly, breaks off from the others and sidles up to me. His arm slips around my waist, a snake encircling its prey, his breath hot and heavy down my neck.

'Come on, you know you want to.' The smirk plastered across his face as offensive as his cologne. 'We're all here for a bit of fun, aren't we?'

Earlier, I might have melted into his arms, thirsty for a white face 5,800 miles from home. *Cheap girl.* The words that Poh-Poh spat at me the night before, their acidity burning me from the inside, ringing in my head. *Cheap, cheap, cheap.*

'Get. Off. Me.' I ram my heel into his foot, a flaring motion of hurt and anger.

'You crazy bitch.' He pushes me against the wall and I lose grip on my phone. I can only watch as it hits the ground. His friends, noticing they're missing one from the pack, come running and pull him away, shooting me half-apologetic looks.

A chill washes over me as I bend down to retrieve my phone. Its glass front is smashed pitifully; only a black screen stares back at me. *Fuck.* A wave of panic rears its head. *It's fine, just get to the hospital.* I look out for the distinctive red taxis that are usually dotted around the roads. When I can't find one, I head towards the stop for my usual bus home to City One. I make my way down the narrow streets, cautious of losing my footing, as the tall buildings close in on me from both sides. Lights flood the roads, an ambush glaring and alarming. The city never sleeps: even as darkness descends, it bursts into electric chaos. Garish neon signs, bright LED billboards, huge flickering screens. *Stay awake*, they scream. *Sleep is for the weak.*

Something doesn't seem right when I get to the bus stop and there isn't a queue. From a distance, a voice projected by a megaphone rises above muffled shouts and chants. Of course. *The god-*

damn protests. I can't think; my mind skips to and fro, struggling for something concrete to grasp. My grandmother is in hospital and I'm stuck an hour's bus journey away with no phone and no bus in sight.

I pace up and down, swatting mosquitoes from my legs. If only I had a car, but no one I know here drives since public transport is supposed to match the efficiency of its citizens. Which leaves the MTR. I shudder. Some things can't be avoided forever, especially not the metro system. Just as I'm looking for directions to the closest station, someone calls my name from behind.

I turn to see Elsie walking towards me. She's swapped her immaculate office attire for a black tee and jeans. 'Thought it was you.' She talks too loudly. 'Changed your mind? Joining us at the protests?'

'No… I, uh…' I falter.

She wrinkles her nose. 'Have you been drinking?'

I need to get to the hospital. She'll know where the station is. Words spill out of me, stumbling over one another, as I explain my predicament. 'Can you help me?' I pause. 'Please.'

I wait for her to make a cutting remark about my inability to take the MTR but the corners of her lips lift into a sympathetic smile. 'Yes, of course. Come with me la.'

We walk side by side. She says, 'My friend told me lots of people have showed up. They're spreading out and blocking traffic from getting to the Cross Harbour Tunnel. That's why there's no bus, no taxi.'

The MTR station comes into sight up ahead and I turn to her, 'I'll figure it out from here. They have maps, right? I better not keep you from the protests.'

She sighs. 'I will come with you. Don't want you getting lost without your phone.'

I'm about to tell her she doesn't have to, that I'll be fine. I'm not sure I want her here but she's already walking away. I catch up to her and we take the escalators down.

The last time I took the MTR was with Poh-Poh. We were running late to meet Uncle Albert for dim-sum because I'd slept in. The platform heaved with people in every direction. As soon as the train arrived, alighting passengers battled against those pushing their way on. Poh-Poh grabbed my wrist as the 'do-do-do' warning noise sounded. The doors began to close, shoving into me. I pulled myself free, wincing at the shooting pain in my shoulders. Reaching for a handhold, I stood sandwiched between Poh-Poh and a sweaty man playing Candy Crush at full volume, trying to avoid the smirks other passengers were giving me. When we got off, we were swallowed into the masses. There was no time to stop and think about where to go. People elbowed their way in between Poh-Poh and I at the escalators, and I watched as she got on and I was still behind. Courtesy was ground into dust here. Eventually, as wrong as it felt, I forced my way through. When I reached the top, Poh-Poh sighed and asked why I was so slow and I swore to myself I'd never take the MTR again.

Now, though, there's room to breathe, left by those who made their way home before the protests erupted. There are no lines to pass through the turnstiles and we wait on a platform that isn't teeming with crowds. Someone bumps into me from behind and I turn to see a little boy looking up at me.

'Aiya!' His grandmother, clutching his large school bag, comes up to us and frowns at him. 'I always tell you not to run around. Say sorry!'

The little boy grabs his grandmother's hand and apologises shyly. I give him a small nod. The train pulls up and we get on, Elsie and I sit on one side and the boy and his grandmother sit opposite us. The boy chatters away, imitating the station announcements, first in Cantonese, then Mandarin, then English. It's after ten but he's still wearing his school uniform, probably heading home from cram school. The pressure cooker that is this city is yet to dampen his spirits. His grandmother nods along, exasperated, as he talks, intercepting only to scold him to sit still and be quiet. Having said all he needs to say, he rests his head against his grandmother's shoulder and closes his eyes. She pats his face gently and then, as if she isn't supposed to, lets a smile emerge as she gazes at her sleeping grandchild.

I picture my Poh-Poh's small, delicate frame in a hospital bed. Tears well in my eyes. Elsie nudges me and tells me we have to get off at Mong Kok. I look away blinking, pretending to fix my contacts.

When we cross the platform and board the next train, Elsie holds out her phone. 'You want to call your family?'

I shake my head. 'I can't remember any of their numbers.'

'Are you close to your Poh-Poh?' The abruptness of her question threatens to revive the tears.

'I can't speak Cantonese that well, so we struggle.' *I should have let her nag me. Oh god, why did I yell at her?* 'Before I moved here, I only saw her every three years or so.' I hesitate for a moment. 'Sometimes it's like we're strangers. I know we shouldn't be but she doesn't understand me. I'm too different from what she knows, I wonder if she even likes me.'

'Don't be silly la. My Poh-Poh died two years ago. I used to think like you when I was younger.' Her eyes take on that faraway look that often accompanies the recall of memories. 'Whenever I was ill, she would say 'It's your own fault. You never listen!' But then she'd make soup and congee. She'd say it was for herself so I didn't pass her my sickness but my bowls were always fullest.'

'But every time she speaks to me, it's to complain or to scold.' The frustration towards Poh-Poh that had been building up last night dissipates, leaving residues of weariness. 'She treats me like a child. 'Where did you go? Why so late? Why aren't you smarter?' My friends' grandmothers, back in England – they're so… soft. All hugs and praise. Not mine.'

Elsie looks at me. Her eyes, usually so haughty, are kind. 'They have a different way of expressing. It's all in here.' She points to the middle of her chest.

Suddenly, I think of how every morning when I wake up, there's always an orange, perfectly peeled, sitting in the fridge for me. Poh-Poh noticed in the first weeks that I left the large oranges she bought untouched. 'Oranges are good for you. Vitamin C,' she said one day, pointing at them with a frown. 'Very sweet. Eat them.' I told her I didn't know how to peel them. 'Aiii, how old are you? Don't know how to do simple things. You're just lazy,' she clicked her tongue at me and went back to watching a melodrama on TV.

The next morning, I found a peeled orange on a plate in the fridge. I didn't eat it, thinking she might be saving it for when she came back from her morning stroll along the Shing Mun River. But that evening when I returned home, she came out of the kitchen as soon as I opened the door. 'Orange peeled for you, and you still don't eat?' Every morning after that, before she left, she would make sure one was ready for me when I woke up. Without fail. Even as the weeks passed and the silences grew prickly. Even as the oranges were sometimes left uneaten and I stopped having dinner with her and returned home later and later.

Until this morning. It was hardly surprising. I heard a noise from her room and thought it odd she hadn't left yet. I contemplated telling her I was sorry for what I said the night before. But I paused outside her door, hand poised to knock, and couldn't find the right words, so I left and took the bus to work. Now, the guilt crawls inside me, questioning why I didn't say something, *anything*.

We change trains again at Kowloon Tong. My throat begs for water and my head aches under the harsh white lights. I just want to get to the hospital. Elsie holds out a tissue. 'Your mascara's smudged.' I take it from her gratefully and dab underneath my eyes.

'Do you like it here?' Her brusqueness throws me off again. I'm not sure what she wants to hear.

'Yes… and no,' I say finally. Her probing eyes ask me for more than a three-word answer. 'It's been… hard at times. I didn't think it would be like this, it's familiar but also so foreign. And I don't really know anyone outside of family and the office.'

'Oh, you're always rushing off after work. We thought you go to meet with friends.'

'Friends, ha.' I look down, rub the hem of my skirt between my fingers.

'You never come to our social events. We wondered if you think you are better than us.' She nudges my arm playfully. 'British-born, overseas university grad, perfect English. Too good for us Hong-Kongers la.'

I shake my head. 'The main reason I moved here was because I couldn't find a job back home.'

'Then come out with us next time, we'll help you get to know

Hong Kong. And you can practise your Cantonese. Everyone's nice, promise. All that talk about HK girls being shallow, only care about money' – she rolls her eyes – 'not all of us are like that.'

'Oh, I know you fight for social justice too,' I flash a grin at her.

'Wah, I was so offended when you questioned what we are really fighting for.' She crosses her arms, a mock-attempt at grievance.

'Well, it just seems like most people are protesting out of hate,' I shrug.

'What, you don't know that Beijing interferes with our elections? Even though they promised to give us autonomy? I don't think you can argue that is okay at all.'

'Yeah but... what about people insisting they're not Chinese, but Hong-Kongese or whatever? Aren't you still *Chinese*?'

'Hong Kong Chinese.' She pauses, then raises an eyebrow. 'But if we are Chinese, then so are you.' An amused look crosses her face. Her point sinks in. I give in and she explains the politics of the protests. This time, I listen. I don't interrupt her, as I did in the office. If anything, I'm glad for the distraction. Our last interchange is at Tai Wai and we stay on the train for two stops before we arrive at City One. She shows me the directions to the hospital on her phone, only a five-minute walk. I thank her for her help.

'It's fine, Cynthia. I hope your Poh-Poh is okay.' She waves me off as I leave the station.

It's nearing eleven o'clock. I hasten my pace into a jog, along a street softly lit with the orange glow of the streetlamps. Beads of sweat line my forehead. I saw a different side to Elsie, I was wrong about her. I was wrong about a lot of things. I'll say sorry to Poh-Poh, I'll find the words this time. I notice Uncle Albert pacing back and forth at the hospital entrance – he's going to be livid I'm late.

I'll try to explain but I doubt he'll listen. I'll let him reprimand me. When he spots me, he comes running and grabs me in his arms. I stand motionless, listening as the proud son of my grandmother sobs over my shoulder.

There are many things that if left unsaid, the other person might not understand. But in this instance, I understand.

I understand.

* * *

I find my mother, paying for packs of incense sticks. I show her the two oranges and together, we return to the apartment. She tells me stories of who my grandmother was before I ever existed. Ever since my mother landed in Hong Kong, she hasn't let herself cry in front of me. My mother is a proud woman. Like her mother.

It's been two weeks since a brain aneurysm ruptured and condemned my grandmother to her death. On that night at the hospital, my whole being was hollow, afloat, only the relentless ticking of the clock keeping me grounded. I returned in the early hours to an empty flat, the guilt pounding in my head. *If only I hadn't shouted at her, if only I had been at home, if only, if only…* Over and over again until I fell asleep. When I woke up, caught in that brief haze when the last tendrils of slumber are yet to release their grip, I was able to forget about her passing – if only momentarily. I wandered over to the fridge to get a drink and inside, on a plate, sat a peeled orange.

The days after that, I took time off work and stayed in the flat, melodrama reruns playing in the background. Elsie came to check on me several times, even bringing me food. Some mornings, I walked along the Shing Mun River, taking the same steps as Poh-

Poh. It struck me how little I knew of her, how we were connected by blood and yet our attachments were stretched so thin. My grief felt wrong somehow, as if I didn't deserve to claim it for myself. I'd grown up only seeing her every few years, so it was like she wasn't actually gone but just in some place 5,800 miles away.

Now, as we prepare for her funeral, her death becomes more real. When I see her body in the coffin and then watch as she is lowered into the ground, I know she has gone. We burn the incense sticks and give the two oranges as offerings. Once people start to leave for the customary post-funeral banquet, I tell my mother and Uncle Albert that I'll catch up later, hugging them both in turn. Together, they walk away, two figures clothed in black, as I kneel down in front of my grandmother's gravestone. Carefully picking up one orange, I press my thumbnail into the skin to make a crack. I pick the skin off in small chunks, pithy peel embedding under my nails. If Poh-Poh were here, she'd swat my hands away – 'Aiii, you're doing it wrong, silly girl' – and do it herself. But she is not here and this is the best I can do. I peel the second orange and arrange them on the plate. The thick smell of incense lingers in the air as I get up, leaving behind all that was unsaid.

INTERVAL TRAINING

Lara Williams

Anna used to be a runner but now she only swam. She swam three times a week. She used to run three times a week, which landed her around a point zero, nervous energy wise. She was hoping swimming might do the same except she only knew breaststroke, which wasn't so great for pounding out anxiety. Front crawl might have worked but she couldn't figure out when to breathe. She'd also tried butterfly, but it seemed so fundamentally inefficient: expending the most amount of energy to do something in the slowest amount of time. Instead she waded expansively through the water; moving like she was awaiting the embrace of a dog that was happy to see her or inviting the waiting staff to join her for a drink.

The pool was an old-fashioned one, with separate baths for men and women, plus a mixed bath. She swam in the mixed bath because she wasn't fucking hysterical. Individual changing rooms lined the sides of the pool. They had heavy wooden doors, which covered you from neck to shin, topped with candy striped curtains. You had to be careful not to squat. She liked the changing rooms, with their cold Victorian tiles and forgivingly eroded mirrors. Sometimes she would find it hard to step outside them, her limbs heavy with disinclination. She would sit on the little bench, her clothes packed inside her handbag, her socks wet, already, and she wouldn't be able to move.

In those moments she took the opportunity to look up on her phone other things that might ease her anxiety. She would Google things that might be making her more anxious: caffeine, Instagram. She would Google things that might make her less anxious: double cleansing, more ostensibly feminist porn. Sometimes she would hold her phone to her ear to listen to a meditation podcast: a podcast that always began by requesting she smooth out her forehead, which was like a hard-to-iron-fabric, once she'd flattened out one part, another bit had bunched up again. She wondered if it was the smoothness of swimming she craved.

In the swimming pool, she did what she called interval training, borrowed from when she ran. Interval training was where you would sprint for a bit and then walk for a bit. It was supposed to increase stamina. In her swimming version, after each slow lap she rewarded herself with a long rest, watching her legs bloat inelegantly beneath the water. Despite what she considered the recent total decrepitation of her body and face, during these rests, men would try to talk to her. They would say things like: 'nice day for it' or: 'that's a pretty swimsuit.' She was grateful for their attention, and only slightly afraid.

In the pool she would swim for as long as she could bear, and then she would be back in the changing rooms, often the same stall; her body damp beneath her clothes, staring at the door. She started taking a book with her, so she had something to read. Once she made a pillow out of her sweatshirt and a blanket out of her towel, lay across the wooden bench and catnapped for an hour. 'It's okay to rest,' the meditation podcast urged. 'Whatever you feel is completely fine for you.'

When Anna was a runner she used to worry a lot about getting murdered. *I hope I don't get murdered*, she used to think, before going for a run. When she got back from a run she thought, *well*

I'm glad I wasn't murdered. Sometimes her thoughts could be a performance. In the swimming pool she only worried about suddenly and violently menstruating, or one of her breasts popping out. But in these scenarios, she was not the victim. And in her little stall she had space for those thoughts: the real ones, the ones that were just for her. Listening to her podcast, she scanned the porcelain tiles: the smile of a toenail come loose from a toe, a dark hair tangled like an ampersand. The changing room was full of assurances.

One of the men in the swimming pool was talking to her more regularly now. He was a lifeguard and he would say things like 'you need to lift your head higher and keep your shoulders level so that you can breathe'; or: 'are you okay?' Sometimes he would tell her when a swimming session was over, his uniform plimsolls level with her face. She would push herself away from the side of the pool, floating backwards. 'What if I don't want to?' she would reply, and pout. Could she be cute anymore? Was that something she could get away with? Could she move to South East Asia and teach English as a foreign language? Did it matter?

The meditation podcast told her all things were possible: whatever you feel is completely fine for you. When she ran she used to listen to things she could also dance to: Prince, Fleetwood Mac, Len. The venn diagram of running and dancing produced a fat, pinched oval of commonality. She wondered what swimming overlapped with: its tedious back and forth.

One evening after the lifeguard had informed her of the end of the swimming session and asked if she would vacate the pool, she did so, hurrying to her favoured stall, removing her swimsuit and putting on her everyday clothes. The same lethargy came over her, compacted by the lifeguard and the podcast: one questioning whether she was okay, the other affirming that she was. And when the lifeguard, or one of the other lifeguards, called to make sure everyone had gone, to their homes or their dinner plans or whatever else people did after an evening spent swimming, she remained silent, her legs crossed up on top of the wooden bench, the door left ajar.

The swimming pool was dark at night, with occasional ponds of light near the windows. Anna left her stall only to use the bathroom, her feet bare against the cold tiles. She was not able to sleep until the very early hours of the morning, but it was a good sleep: the sort of sleep you are only capable of once you have progressively relaxed every muscle in your body, while mindfully deepening your breathing.

She was awoken by a sound: something like a noisy kitchen in a high class restaurant. She leaned over to open the door just a touch. Beside the swimming pool were long tables covered with white linen tablecloths. On top of the tables were large bouquets of flowers and bottles of champagne cooling in metal buckets filled with ice. In the corner was a three-tiered cake. The pool itself had been drained, the water replaced with rows of seating and a central aisle. She pushed the door to and tried smoothing out her forehead, which at this point might as well have been nylon or silk.

Inside the changing room stall she heard all the many stages of a wedding: the ceremony, the photographs, the speeches, the dancing. Every now and again she allowed herself a glimpse of the action, everything happening in the now drained pool. She was relieved to see something take its place: something that couldn't be contained, something naive if not ultimately hopeful. Towards the end they played a song she recognised from her running playlist, possibly Prince. She wondered whether to move.

DISTRACTION

Stephanie Victoire

A man with Tourette's walks past me twice, a smile first and then, 'I found you!' his tic says on the second turn. What a perfect phrase to escape a person's mouth. *I'm glad you've found me because I've been looking for myself*, I think in response. I wind the film on and place the lens cap back onto my Canon. I finally decided I'd finish the reel today; the first half of it is taken up with mistakes and people whom I did know, but have so quickly become strangers again. Sat in the camera for nearly a year, I must get them out. Walking the streets, I look for moments to steal that can't ever be mine, faces that will never have names. I take comfort in the things I am able to see from a distance.

In the street I get compliments on my hair and my coat, both are too big and fluffy I suddenly feel; I am taking up too much space for my liking. I'm used to shrinking; I have become excellent at slipping through walls over the years, and most times I really did want to disappear. The walls of London are unforgiving though – spray-paint toxic and pissed-on, angry and tall. But they'll always be here holding in my ghosts for me. Ghosts come out more in the night – everyone knows that, and I am coaxed out with them, entranced in my own dance macabre.

They can still stir in the daylight. They whisper to me in smells to get my attention. From the corner of King's Cross underpass, the scent of dying roses and cider dried into fabric grabs me by the elbow and drags me ten years back – into the toilet cubicles of Camden pubs and the student union bar we would sack off Drama lectures for. Drama was horseshit. We were there to write, we wanted words not performance. We wanted to intoxicate; we wanted to fuck with ourselves and anyone else who felt like us – without the spotlight. But we never seemed to want to go home. With bags carrying our books, tobacco and the A4 pads we practiced our voices on, we'd walk and walk – sometimes in circles – staying out to find the smoky, decaying places to fit into.

Poorly lit corners of Soho were the best for secret self-harm, trembling fingers holding a roll-up in the damp and the cold, the other hand shoved into a rough denim pocket, rubbing burns into the wrist out of anxiety. Anna seemed to sniff out the ones who also damaged themselves in response to love. She found me on our very first day, signing up for Eighteenth Century Fiction. She made me feel less attractive and I made her feel more wrong, but we laughed too much together to care about the toxicity. We created a world around us that was beautiful, taping up pretty things on the inside walls of our bubble with dirty plasters. We'd dress up and take photos in her garden, write poetry and hide in galleries.

One night I saw her kiss her girlfriend at the time on Greek Street while I struggled to look correct standing next to her band-mates. I'd never seen such dizziness between two people in reality before. With my heart drowned in red wine and Jägerbombs, my limited vision took in the streams of beauty. Against that attractive nonchalance, sitting under black eyeshadow and sticky skin, I felt like something else to these women I didn't dare call new friends. I ignored myself around them because I thought they were ignoring me too. But inside the venue, when the amps were plugged in and the feedback and fuzz hit the walls, we could all ignore everything, and we were the same. Stomping out the anxiety and bouncing our pints up and down in their plastic cups, that music entered the bloodstream quicker than cocaine. It gave the courage to kiss, to thrust the body into the protruding hip bones of someone else who was just as thin because of art – let's tangle our bones together in raging expression.

I make my way on the 73 bus towards good places to take photographs. I hop off by Store Street to cut up to Tottenham Court Road. I ride the current, heading in the direction of Leicester Square, into that very past that looks so good in 35mm film. On the way, a ghost sneaks up on me with a chalky scent and a song I once learned on the guitar; I remember practising those four sweet, simple little chords so I could sing about having the time of my life. A worn but hopeful man in a camouflage jacket sitting on the pavement gives as much desire for the song to be true as I once did. I slow down as I walk past him, smiling at the cigarette hanging out of his mouth while he sings. He winks at me and I feel at home in his meaning.

Two quid lighter but one perfect image loaded, I walk away from him wondering if I should have just lived like this instead, never having tried to befriend the beauty. Clouds cut into the light by the Underground and I lower the shutter speed to take in the woman who's delighted to see her friend, seems as though they haven't seen each other for a long time; I am grateful for their smiles brightening the frame. I then remember that there is a piano down in the station. I descend to get my shot, though no one is playing it today. But there is a space at that seat for a ghost who used to make me laugh until I cried, who filled me up with music I didn't know, smelling of butterscotch, bourbon and sweet herbs.

His accent gave off the heat it was born in, charming anyone into dabbing their brows and craving a cold glass of lemonade. Always making sure I'd never spend an evening feeling lonely, he pulled me out, pushed my edges and encouraged me onto a dancefloor and into the mouths of women so I could have my own adventures alongside him. He was never coy about the men he was sure to take home when we said our goodnights, even though the sun was always just about rising when we stopped dancing. But no matter how drunk we were, he always made me explain my route home to him so that he knew where I was supposed to be.

Only in the city for a couple of years, he took to calling me his best friend. I watched him get his heart broken and he watched me lick the wounds of my outstretched arms and we did our best to giggle through it. In the queue at G-A-Y one warm night, we talked about how he was going to say no to the person he'd fallen madly in love with because the possibility of him reaching happiness seemed karmically untrue. I wanted to convince him that he was more than worthy of it, but there was nothing you could say that would ever change Noah's mind once he'd made it. For the rest of the night we talked about a co-written memoir we'd put together one day about the summer we both fell in love then died. We were good at making things funny through our tears.

Close to where we were stood, musing and riffing, I tried to ignore the set of steps where Danny and I once talked about why he couldn't love me and why despite myself, I had to love him. But that ghost doesn't belong here; it lives in Elephant and Castle where I haven't been since 2010 because that ghost knows how to cripple me. If I think about it, the smell of a Wetherspoons carpet and wet brick gets stuck in my lungs. I am in those sheets again, with a hand around my throat, fucking for hours to Deftones. I developed the craft of looking the other way with him. Stomachs shrunken on Ecstasy, ear pins lost under the pillow and the blinds keeping out the afternoon sun, we were deliciously coming undone, Danny and I. He was a pretty boy with lots of hair, well-kept lips and eyelashes that fluttered shadows against neon lights. I was the one he chose and that was enough for me to be kept waiting for him there for an hour outside the station, watching cars twirl the roundabout until they turned to madness in my sight.

He asked me to be his girl that night; he waltzed me down Walworth Road and told me he was officially off the market. We tripped through the playground we had to walk through to get to his house, swimming in Kronenbourg and an unbelievable love. At the time I was deliriously happy and everyone else hated him. He was a frozen husk in front of other people and it seemed only I could thaw him out in his own bed. But I could never wait to get back into that room where I let him, and the sound of guitar distortion, pull the room apart.

I sit down to have a cigarette directly in front of a 'Girls, Girls, Girls' sign and shoot the camera at it without adjusting the aperture; things in Soho often don't occur in focus. I have an image of Anna come to me suddenly, standing in the middle of the street at three in the morning, her teary eyes and streetlights blurring the picture in my mind. It was her birthday and we had spent the night in a rock pub with a late licence we loved round the back of Oxford Street that isn't there anymore. She was saying too much that night, almost as though she were trying to give evidence she was broken, which often happened when the wine kept coming, the hours got smaller and people stuck around long enough to listen.

There was a small handful of us, though enough to create a presence around the table. The only other person I knew was Caleb, our mutual friend from Uni. He'd brought his girlfriend along: the first time either of us had met her. I tried earnestly to get to know her but was distracted from her careful Scandinavian accent by Anna, who kept saying, with her sweet-sour alcohol breath deep into my ear, that she wanted to fuck her.

It took Caleb a lot longer to see Anna and I for who we really were as if he didn't want to believe that he could have found better people to hang out with. He'd witnessed us argue in the canteen once when our separate foul moods happened to clash. And he'd humoured us over lunch at Café Boheme under the guise of discussing a literature project he'd joined us for. But Anna did the usual thing of making black comedy out of everything he considered of value. She enjoyed her role of cryptic fuck-toy, letting her slip-dress ride up into the groove of her hip and stroking her hair up away from her neck as she stretched before him with an apathetic look on her face. He still never truly got it, even though I do believe he liked us, and we did like him. But he was completely oblivious to the fact that whilst he was celebrating his strange-but-cool friend's birthday, she was plotting and willing to destroy him and his relationship in an instant.

But the truth was she had real feelings for her straight friend, Molly, who was also there that night. Molly seemed sensible and sweet and wouldn't rot the way Anna really liked them at all. I was relieved Molly had come to her senses and saved herself by pulling away from an unhealthy hug, black eyeshadow mixed with tears, pasted on her shoulder. *'Don't leave,'* Anna pleaded with her, realising her friends had all seen too much of her for one night. Molly could feel the peril that was possible: the sabotage of her relationship with her boyfriend, time that might be consumed by fragile conversations and overwrought texts. Molly was effectively running away, that taxi could not have left quick enough. But no matter how damaging everything was at the time, I couldn't leave her standing there crying in the street on her birthday. She was too far from home, so I took her back to mine.

I had my own agenda for avoiding loneliness that night, for Danny had had his phone switched off for days. Nursing hangovers apparently, with people he would never tell me the names of. I appear to have a knack for loving those who can't seem to feel it on the inside. Always standing on the outer casing of their hearts, I speak into them my confessions in the hope that a crack of light will emerge. I catch myself in the reflection of a Transit van driving past, attempting to see myself as they saw me. I've never been able to get self-portraits right with the camera; I shall be no Vivian Maier – I am lost in mirrors, not found.

I decide to take my final frame before it pisses it down with rain. Standing at the corner of Old Compton and Dean, I open up the distance so I can capture down the way, a corridor of ghosts. Shot number thirty-six may be all or nothing, but I take it anyway, for old times' sake. For the belly-laughter, the half-eaten shared chow meins, the mushroom spores carried in jacket pockets, the sitting on the curb before sunrise, the songs sang with strangers, the crushes never meant for anything else. The smell of coffee and rosemary shampoo rushes to the back of my throat until I can taste it. I savour it for a moment before the dirty cloud above me rumbles his warning.

I wind the film on until it hits the wall and can move on no more.

BUT NOT LIKE THAT

Susan James

Men from the village would sometimes walk up the track to the farm at night. Sarah and I would lie in bed with our eyes shining like moons listening as they'd circle the property, drunk: rattling barn doors, throwing clods of mud at one another, tapping at the sitting room window, making sexualised sounds in high-pitched voices. Sarah would feel her way out of the bed in the darkness, reaching for the handle of the cricket bat next to the door. I'd lie rigid, cold at the sudden absence of her beside me. We'd wait for them to leave before speaking, before relief manifested itself into steaming, boiling tea made on the camping stove. Nothing was ever taken or broken that I can remember. Farmhands who thought us living together was a side-show, something that was both titillating and yet deeply offensive. If only they'd have seen Sarah in her long-johns, wearing her blankets like a coronation robe, ready to thwack them with a stick.

We slept in the same bed because there was no electricity, no running water and their intrusion did nothing to convince us that we needed a man. Of course, that was a long time ago.

* * *

Half-stooping, I shift the bundle of fodder from one shoulder to the other as the snow creaks, compacting under my heels as I walk up to the high field. Sky and valley seamlessly smudge one into the other. Only the dry-stone walls squaring off the fields below are visible from up here. The heavens are a low-white ceiling, so pregnant with winter that I can almost reach up to touch them.

'Spinster is an awful word.' I say to Marigold, my favourite heifer, as I drop the fodder onto the ground. The beast is miserable but she dips her head, shaking it emphatically side-to-side and exhaling small white clouds that I take as an acknowledgement. I run my hand along the animal's back and tuck my chin into the knot of the headscarf pressed against my neck.

'Awful word.' I say again, because then it comes to me that it's written on Sarah's death certificate which was one of the papers that I'd pulled out of the kitchen drawer for sorting. Marigold chews loudly, her jaw swinging in a circle and her tongue thick and pink and warm. I can't stay up here for long but I need to catch my breath a moment. I need to give my old windchime bones a chance at resting.

The stream at the side of the house has been frozen for two days. Three thumps with an old tree branch has temporarily cracked the glaze over the top, but it's left my arms aching, a strange detached pain that makes simply hanging my hands at my sides an effort. The shock of it: the thought of my own sixty-seven years is greater than the cold water against my skin.

'I've had a visitor,' I tell Marigold, clapping my hands together to warm them. She keeps her head down. Of course, she already knows this story. There's been no one for a month or so but the cows don't seem to mind hearing the same story twice, three or even five times, and Marigold doesn't move away even as the snow catches the corners of her eyes, making them water.

I used to talk to the cows the way that a mother might talk to a baby: saying silly things in silly voices about nonsense, really. Sarah was the same. We did it to all the animals: the baby-talk. Of course, there are fewer now. The dogs and cats are long buried and the cows and bullocks have almost all disappeared to market. I still speak to Marigold and Rumi and Mary, but things are different now. I use the voice that I use when speaking to people as if I think the beasts will reply. It's nice to hear the noise of my own narration, putting sounds to the words running through my head. I don't say anything else to Marigold. She's miserable in this weather, and I'm tired of telling her that she should be happy it's not sleeting. And anyway, we're all miserable up here and always will be in the winter.

* * *

Sarah wasn't supposed to stay forever. But forty years turned out to be almost forever. She'd been sleeping in a cow shed on the neighbouring farm whilst the property was empty, and it was the end of the war and well, you could never tell what some people had been through, and we started talking. My father was ailing, and I wasn't sure what would happen to the farm when he died. Fifty acres but the house was run-down, the outbuildings barely standing, you could count the herd on a single hand, but Sarah seemed happy to help, grateful for work and for a warmer place to sleep. She said she was going to join a convent. Temporary or not, when she arrived, she hammered silver crucifixes into the wall above the bed and over the fire in the sitting room. Looking back, it suggests a permanence that neither one of us was prepared for. Forty years is a long time to live with someone and not be able to remember what it was that made them stay. She wanted to live in a convent, but I'm the one paying penance now.

I was an only child and a shy one. Life on the farm without siblings or young cousins hadn't given me the practice of making friends, sharing things, but Sarah had a way of giving back and we settled into that first Autumn together as if we'd always intended to. I think despite what was said in the village, we must take some responsibility for our own isolation. The farm became her convent: a way to isolate herself from her own feelings and from temptation. The farm was my home, too, and I wasn't sure when I was supposed to leave. Sarah and I shared a bed, but it wasn't like that.

* * *

It's a slow walk away from Marigold and back to the house, shuffling against a wind that's galloping from one side of the field to the other, trying to turn me in circles, inside out. Headscarf pulled tightly under my chin, head bent, eyes to the snow, I lead with the crown of my head for home.

Sarah and I shared a bed, but I wasn't like that.

The farmhouse door is stiff, swollen by the cold and wet and difficult to open. I stagger backwards when it swings wide, and stamping the snow from my boots, call out in habit to the cat who no longer answers, but it sounds good to fill the house with a voice. I close the door; the wind follows me inside.

* * *

Estelle, that is her name. I've been trying to remember all the way from the high field. Estelle is the lady who's going to help me sell the farm and find a cottage in the village. She'd walked up the drive in her skirt and heels, apologised for being late, said it was because she didn't want to bring the company car up the dirt track to the drive. Sarah would have hated her, and the way the woman's perfume had filled the room. I imagined my friend as a vengeful spirit: I could smell the wet grass coming off Sarah's boots under the table. Estelle's hands had been too big to properly drink her tea. Cupping the cup between her palms, she'd ignored the bone China handle, reminding me of how my Grandfather would sip gravy from the stew basin and earn a telling off from his wife.

Sarah and I went to a Christmas dance in the village hall a few months after she'd moved in. We picked out dresses from my mother's wardrobe, sewing the hems shorter because there was no one to tell us not to. Sarah drove my father's old car down the driveway and out onto the lane and down towards the smattering of cottages with their chapel and pub and grocer, butcher, post office and baker. We stayed an hour and sat alone. I stood up to dance but once I started everyone took their seats, talking in half-circles to each other as I stepped from one foot to the other, alone. When I waved at Sarah to join me, she shook her head and curled her hands just like the tiny fists of Jesus still nailed to the cross, nailed to the bedroom wall at home.

* * *

There was a time when coming back inside in the winter felt like a relief; Sarah waiting for me with a cup of boiling black tea and a slice of thick white buttered bread. She always had a way with fire and in the winter, it was always burning. Coal was the one luxury we allowed for. Even in summer, she smelt of smoke. Now, I fetch my own tea, start my own fires and butter my own bread. If I keep my coat on for long enough, leave the fire burning, then I'll start feeling my fingers and feet.

The spit-crackle in the grate forces me to lower my shoulders, to let my stomach settle over the waistband of my trousers, makes my wrists sag over the arms of the chair. Tomorrow, there'll be a delivery and I'll have to be early, be quick or it'll be sopping wet. Every four weeks, it's left on the dry-stone wall next to the gate, on the lane, a selection of food stuffs: butter, lard, cheese, eggs, bread, tinned meat, tomatoes. Coal comes separately in the Autumn. Fresh bread comes once a week in the spring and summer but now I have to make do with less. It used to be enough.

I'm bone-tired, weary beyond words and when I close my eyes for a moment, I'm half-floating, mind swirling away and out of my head, up the chimney and through the top of the house and out into the cold. I'll sit here for a beat longer and settle the warmth back into my blood.

* * *

Sarah died three months ago halfway up the high field. It was immediate. The doctor had said so. I'd been sweeping the yard between the outbuildings, assuming she'd slipped inside behind me but when the sky started bruising, I realised she was missing, but even then, I hadn't felt any sense of danger, any forewarning. I didn't quickly settle my feet into my shoes, and I didn't leave the cup of tea that I'd made. I dallied, I dawdled until I walked up to see for myself and saw her lying in the grass and I had to walk a mile to the next farm over. Neighbours we'd never said a word to, but who had a telephone, who thank God made the call. I didn't think it would do for me to be screaming.

'Sarah always said you'd have to carry her out of here in a box,' I'd said to Estelle, 'And she was right.'

There's a skin of cobwebs hanging off the corner of the Welsh dresser. Strange how a visitor can make you see your home differently. Yellow, brittle newspapers tied in twine, stacked under the armchairs. The bag of food hanging from a hook on the wall to stop the mice from eating. How obvious the seams in the wallpaper are now, sheets hung by my father many decades before. I'd promised Estelle that I'd make a start on tidying things up. Some things have been easy: old paperwork and bedding that had grown heavy and black with damp. I've opened up cupboards, some which had been closed for years, revealing the artefacts of someone else's life: my father's spectacles, a book of my mother's recipes, a handwritten inventory of the seasonal workers who'd once worked alongside my father, many of whom I can't remember, but whose names I recognise from the memorial in the village and who I know died in the Great War. It seems both a cruelty and a kindness that it's been left to me to sort through, re-live and then dispose of everything. It's exhausting, and easily put off for later. And whilst there's things I can take with me when I leave, I cannot take the view from the window or the way the light dances over the stream, dappling, rippling as if it is being painted by hand. Or the animals that I've reared, grown fat, grown to love.

'And you never married?' I'd noticed the ring on Estelle's finger: the slim golden band that to me, unfairly, seemed an assumption of property. I'd already told her that Sarah and I had lived together, but not like that.

We never had much money. Farm work is hard work. Harder than it had any right being, really. We took to it, though. The two of us, often in silence, digging, pulling the cattle to the high field, rebuilding in the spring what the winter so easily destroyed. Old friends of my father's would take our cattle to market. No place there for a single woman. When my father was ailing and almost certain to die, it had been assumed that I'd start looking for a husband. Without my permission, but also without my denial, it was acknowledged that I would want a man to share the labour, the fire and the bed.

One man came close, but only because he was the only one to walk up the track and onto our property. Charlie McGregor had been a farmhand some years before my father had died. He was ten years older than I was and had a brooding, silent fury in the way he did things: he'd slam a door even on a summer morning, slap the bonnet of a car before getting in; he'd narrow his eyes if you said anything contrary to a country way of thinking. His own family had owned a property on the other side of the dale but it had been sold and the family had rented a cottage in the village, never really adjusting to a life away from the land but instead made soft by it, and Charlie's temper must have grown. He thought he had the feel of this place and us. He'd come around unannounced some evenings but his advances were half-hearted, token gestures to see how close he could get. I wasn't against marriage but it seemed a ridiculous thing to enter into for the sake of it. Sarah and I had been running things just fine. Although, neither of us had appreciated how dreadful the winters could be. We had to try to soothe his ego, placate what he believed to be a slight against him. He said what we were doing was unnatural, and a few weeks later we started getting those night time visits. You can imagine the sort of thing a man like that might say to others to hide his own shame. I told him, I told them, and I'm telling you, Sarah and I shared a bed, but not like that.

Idle gossip gave Sarah the convent she wanted. And I didn't much object either. This was, after all, my home and the only one I'd ever known: the stones placed upon one another by my Grandfather, the blankets we slept under were knitted by his sister; the knives in the kitchen had buttered the bread since my mother was a child. Our bed was the one I'd been birthed in. It was home. The labouring was honest. The slander, concerns and words of others couldn't travel further than the dale. And once we stopped noticing, the unpleasantness lifted like a fog and we gave it almost no thought at all. Although, I am giving it plenty of thought now.

* * *

The days are too short in the winter. The sun sets before four if it's risen at all. The blankets are warm but heavy, a pressing weight that makes standing difficult. My skin is goosey, and my hands shake. I am tired.

This will be my last winter in this house, on this land. I can't bear the thought of what could happen if it isn't: the day when two small food boxes lie rotting on the dry-stone wall, an old woman doing the same thing inside.

'It'll be nice in the village,' Estelle had said. 'plenty of people you'll know and friends for company.'

Hopefully, new faces, younger people. Those who know how to dance.

'And all the mod-cons,' she'd said, glancing around the sitting room.

And I'd quite like an electric fire, too. And not to smell of coal and smoke as if I'm living in a railwayman's yard.

It'll be hard though, I've told her, to live pressed up to someone else's dividing walls, to hear voices through the windows, and to keep noticing the passing of cars. And to have to leave that view: the half-moon hanging over the water, fields folded loosely between hill and sky. But oh, I think, leaning back into the chair as the wind whips against the roof and snowflakes settle deeper into the grass, it'll be very grand in the village now most of them are too old or too dead; it'll be very grand indeed to leave here and to start again.

THE LADY'S NOT FOR BURNING

Sarvat Hasin

The first thing she hated about the House was the walls. Zafar said he would paint them but seven months later, he hadn't even begun. A pale creeping yellow wallpaper in the kitchen and living room. As the sun went down, it turned green, sickly and soft and the shapes on it, like wilting flowers, sea-like and creaturely. A ghastly red in the bedroom, vulgar and bright. It embarrassed her. Next year, if they could afford it, her parents would come to visit her and she couldn't imagine showing them this House – the bordello bedroom, the ugly wallpaper, the carpets that smelled of damp and covered every inch of floor – even the bathroom, which she was sure was unsanitary.

Zafar had lived there a year and a half before her. He'd bought the House fully furnished and these abominations did not seem to offend him. Lubna thought a lot about what her mother would say about this – about the sofas with the floral patterns that weren't theirs but inherited, sofas that once held bodies of strangers. Her mother would be horrified: 'You don't know who's been in them!' But Zafar was so proud of the place, which meant something different to him than it did to her. She sensed but could not fully understand this – when he spoke about the places he'd lived when he'd first come to this country, she knew it was supposed to be impressive – the squalor of the flats, four men to one bathroom, chips for dinner every night. He was the first of his cousins to own a house – Bilal and Muzafar were still renting, even further out of the city than him. The House was where he felt happiest and it was a mutual appreciation – she could feel it opening around him, softening when he came in, the harsh lights dimming to a warm sunny glow as they welcomed their Master. It sat around him comfortably, like a crown.

She, on the other hand, had never felt comfortable here. Lubna arrived with two suitcases of clothes the year that she'd lived in the House. She'd slept only fitfully – her legs danced and jerked in the night. When she got bored of lying there in the dark, waiting for the sun to come up, for Zafar's alarm to go off, she began to clean in the middle of the night. She couldn't vacuum or do the laundry, so she swept instead or read books or ate cereal. She smoked Zafar's cigarettes in the back garden. They tasted harsh and fiery in her throat. The moon howled down at her and everything was quiet, so much quieter than it had been at home, where the whirring of nighttime traffic and her father's loud snores reached every room. Her parent's flat was in the commercial district, upstairs from a dhaba. Street lamps and headlights flashed in through the windows all night, a bright glowy halo in every room.

In the flat garden here, she watched only the moon. Zafar said they lived in the city but it did not feel that way where they were, out in the vast sprawl with its low set houses, broad parks and trees leaning into the leafy streets. Their House was painted an eggy cream. If she went out to the corner store to pick up milk in the mornings, it seemed to wilt out of sight as she walked back up the street, as if retreating from her, turning concave, hiding wickedly behind its neighbours. Even now, she walked up and down the road a few times before she spotted it. Green door. A light blinking on the first floor like a naughty child.

* * *

From the first day, I hated her diligent uselessness. When her husband left for work, she sprung out of bed and began cleaning, even though the House was not dirty – her husband was a neat man, had prepared it nicely for his bride. Even though the carpets were clean, she went at them like a demon. She cooked every morning, even if there were leftovers in the refrigerator. Vile sputtering smells, onions dancing in the pan, shaggy in red and yellow powders – turmeric, chilli, others she retrieved from small glass jars that stained my counters. The freezer was full of these concoctions, heavy glass dishes filled to the brim. The drawers sloshing as she crammed them in.

Her small brown hands, square fingered and greasy, working over my floors, fussing with my net curtains, smoothing down the covers of my bed. She was built small, only five feet tall, and yet seemed to spread around the rooms, seemed to be everywhere at once, filling them with her smells – the oils she rubbed into her hair, sickly sweet perfume, talcum powder patted into her skin, fried spices: her smell moving like a feast from one room to the other, smearing itself on the walls.

Even the plates, chosen for their blue willow patterns, were yellowing under her food. When she'd finally exhausted herself with fussing, she would sit in the living room and turn the television on. The news bleeding into daytime soaps and back again and the woman sitting with her back to it, reading mystery novels she pulled off my shelf. Her fingers all over my Agatha Christies. If I had blood to boil, it would be going then.

* * *

Zafar left the House to a thunderstorm. He was going to a conference in Bristol overnight. She'd never slept alone anywhere before – back in Pakistan, there were six of them. She shared a room until she came here, replacing the sound of her sister's whirring breath with Zafar's gentle snores.

The windows shook, sky cracked with thunder. She ate in front of the television like a child, pouring milk over cornflakes for dessert. Goodness Gracious Me was on. It could be nice to be on her own, both more grownup and innocent than she'd imagined. Zafar liked to look at her while they ate, while they sat around in the evenings watching television. Without his attention, she felt her legs sprawling beneath her, her muscles easing into the chairs. Even if she hated the House, she could learn perhaps to like her own company, even at night. She was finished with her cereal and tilting the bowl of cold milk into her mouth when the lights went off.

Her hands stilled around the bowl. All she could hear was rain. Back home during the power cuts, they knew where every candle was, could reach each torch by memory. They knew their house in the dark as well as by light. She and her family would play cards by candlelight or sing to each other or listen to the radio. It wasn't so bad all together though they complained about it often. Even during the summer, when it was too hot to sleep without the fan, they would drag their mattress out onto the roof and sleep under the stars. The windows flickered with lights from the street. Here, the windows were black with night and streaks of rain.

She got up, bowl in hand, and went to the window. Theirs was the only house with lights off. The floorboards creaked loudly around her, like a child gnashing its teeth. The upstairs light flickered on and off. It was the middle of the night where her parents were and there was no one else she could call on the phone.

Outside the weather rasped on. Lubna stood by the front door till morning, poised to run.

* * *

I started with her tea. Swapped out sugar for salt – childish, small. Watched her wince in the cold dark glass of the window and stifled a laugh in the curtains. She didn't like my House any more than I liked her. I heard her complaining about it to her husband about little things: the milk turning sour overnight – or sometimes quicker than that. I would curdle it after she poured his tea so it was disgusting when she came to her own. I enjoyed her stupid incomprehension at these things. I'd play with the lights when he was out, trying to catch her on her own. I played the floorboards like they were keys on a piano, grew around her closet like mold.

At first she'd tell him, the husband who spent all his days in the office and came home tired and patient but helpless. He loved my House. He always had. I watched him admire its fine walls, its lion's face knocker, when he came home every evening. Eventually, she swallowed these grievances every time.

I thought from the turn of her mouth, her plump displeasure, that I could break her.

For the next few weeks, everything was fine. Everything was easier with Zafar around. He seemed to bring back good weather. He stamped damp feet into the door, brought leaves and twigs into their home like the great outdoors. His shoulders stooped down to hug her. It was the first time they'd been apart since their wedding and she found herself swept up, comforted by his warmth, by how easily he unwrapped his outdoor layers and worked his way to the kitchen, shedding newspapers and bags in the hallway. She watched him eat daal and rice out of the Tupperware in the fridge standing up. It was as if she was witnessing how he must have lived before her, when alone with the House. He nodded at the clock in the living room as if to an old friend.

They held hands as they watched the news, affection and safety bound up in each other. It was a late sunset, the lamps glowed warmly and fingers of dying light touched the House.

Lubna allowed herself to feel a cautious comfort, uncoiling a little. Zafar's hand was warm too. The day had been beautiful. She had slept only the afternoon before he arrived, her dreams racked with images of the House closing in on her. The ceilings were lower than her parents' house – she felt them pressing down against her when she laid in bed, their heavy ancient musk on her chest. But with Zafar, it was simpler – he seemed to expand the room around him. That night, he reached for her and she felt struck by how much she'd been anticipating it – usually their sex had been led by him. Tonight, her hands wandered over him, tugging him into her with a hunger for closeness that hadn't been in the room before. A night apart made all the difference. They rocked the bed in the glow of the moon.

It was only as he rolled off her that she felt it – something creeping around her ankles, a cold rough tug as if trying to drag her out of the bed. Her body sprung upright.

A tension swirling anew. They were not alone.

* * *

The House belonged to my grandfather and then my father and then my brother and when they died it belonged to me.

The wallpaper was mine and the china was mine. When I was a girl, we never used the front room. Only Christmas and Easter. It smelled like pipe smoke and potpourri, a stale stillness. Even when my parents had people over for dinner, things moved slowly – white tablecloth, beautiful set of food, everybody frozen around it as if posing for a painting. When my brother got married, it was the only party we ever had in that house. He wore a blue suit and spilled wine on the carpet but everyone was too happy to care. He and his wife died in a plane crash over the Pacific Ocean, their bodies never recovered. Our parents were ten years gone already, so the House came to me. I moved back in from my bedsit in Clapham, with my things. They'd gutted the place – Henry and his wife had turned it into a modern home. A low green couch instead of the Chesterfield. Every ornament wrapped away in the attic, the Victoriana lamps, the portrait of the Queen, lace doilies, family photographs, glass apples, candlesticks.

On my first night, I brought them down and out of their boxes. A warm July evening. I blew the dust off and built it up again. When the sun came up, I ate breakfast sitting in my father's place at the table. I listened to the morning news on the radio.

* * *

There were rats in the wall. Zafar didn't believe her. She lay awake all night hearing them putter in the architecture. She smelled droppings which Zafar could not, found teeth marks in the walls and in the wrapping paper she used to line their drawers, in the chopsticks that came with their Chinese takeaway but were never used.

Her sleep torn through one night, something damp and hot on her face. Rats in their bed. Eyes like cartoon darts in the dark. When she woke Zafar, they were gone and his face gave away that he didn't believe her. Even the teeth marks, he dismissed: either harmless mice or wear and tear that she could convince him was malignant.

* * *

For fifty years I was alive in the House. I walked to the corner of the street every morning, picked up milk, eggs and the newspaper. I never had it delivered. The exercise was good for me.

The change had not come slowly, it crawled upon us like a plague from the Old Testament. They came through like lightning – first the corner shop, then a flat on the top of the street and more and more and more until every other house on the street was one of theirs. Filling it with their voices, their loud drawling tongues, their orange streaked food, their music and inability to understand us. I couldn't easily buy a pack of cigarettes in the shop anymore.

The new owner, chestnut-skinned and unintelligible, too young to run a shop or brush his hair. I saw him looking at me. They all did. I could feel their eyes like bullets as I walked down the street – even though my skirts never went much higher than my knees but it must have been more than they could see on their wives, who lived in baggy sacks and covered their heads like nuns. I never married nor was ever really serious about anybody. There was a man for a little while in my twenties who seemed like he might stick around but he joined the army and left. There was a man for a while in my thirties but he died before Henry. Never before had I minded not having a husband but I thought about wearing Mummy's ring when I went out – though they would know soon enough anyway, these local leeches who hung around everywhere. I began locking the windows and doors every night.

It is a terrible thing not to feel safe in your own home. And now here she was, carrying another one. I knew before she told her mother or even her husband. Could feel it light up inside her like a cheap ornament. Building in her belly like a fire.

* * *

She asked her mother for prayers. Took out her tasbeeh and sat with it in the rocking chair, turning the beads in her fingers and whispering prayers while Zafar slept until even that didn't feel safe, the chair too animated beneath her body, as if it possessed its own violence.

Lubna had never been scared before. Of all her cousins, she was the brave one. She was the one to stay in the dark room the longest, with the bear rug in their uncle's house. She was the one who told their grandmother when her favourite vase had been destroyed in a game of hide and seek. She was the first to go to college on her own, the first to get a job, the first to get married and leave the country.

She came on a plane all on her own, through the skies into a foreign country to live with a man she'd only met twice before. A house couldn't scare her. The thought was absurd.

* * *

It was getting harder to trick her. The woman was alert – nothing so simple as moving a chair beneath her was going to catch her out. She moved through the House with her eyes peeled open. Not a stray floorboard could catch her out – especially in the day.

So it had to be at night. She was going down to get some milk. Her mother had suggested it over the phone when she heard her daughter wasn't sleeping. Warm milk. I heard them talking about it, mixing turmeric into it as if that could solve anything. This strange voodoo they thought would protect and ease them.

Down the stairs
midnight pitch dark
one foot then the other
a cautious tread
tried to turn on the light
but I shut it
clutching for the bannister
halfway down, feeling safer
more confident
lighter of foot

A step disappeared.

I turned the light back on so he could find her sprawled on the bottom of the stairs.

* * *

When she lost the baby, she knew something had to change. She prayed till her mouth was dry. She gave money in her name and Zafar's, in the name of their unborn child. None of it worked.

Really, it was a shame because there were things she liked about where they lived – not the House, but the street. The people she was getting to know, who sent flowers and brought food when they heard about the baby. A neighbour who began to come regularly, teaching Lubna to crochet. The garden, which was clean somehow, free of the House. Where there were wild roses and a bird feeder. A few weeks ago, as a way of cheering her up, Zafar took her out to the theatre. They got the tube into the centre of town and Lubna wore lipstick for the first time since the baby and sat in a dark room while a man in an opera mask dragged a boat out on stage and a chandelier swung into the audience. Her eyes felt as big as moons on the way home, wide and wondrous. Zafar held her hand through the glittering streets. This life, she thought, was worth keeping, worth fighting for. It became clear what had to be done.

* * *

I died in the loft. I was pulling down the winter duvets when my foot caught on the ladder – really, I shouldn't have been up there but there was no one else to do it so I did it myself. I fell off and down the whole flight of stairs. It was on impact, pretty painless. Not a terrible way to go.

I was born in that House too, a full circle journey, a stamp of belonging. I was never a traveller in anyone else's life, anyone else's home.

She did it while he was away because he would have never allowed it. The husband, I knew, was a careful man, a respectful man. Someone who appreciated the place in life he'd risen up to. He took care of the House and so of me. It was all fine until she came around. Until it began to feel their occupation would be permanent.

A glug of oil down the back. Clever because I couldn't stop her. When she lit the match, I wanted to scream – billowed open all the doors and windows and made them clang like hellfire. It was a still night, no breeze. The fire caught quickly. Somehow the whole street slept until I was up in flames, me and my home withering up to a crisp. She must have put a spell on them. She stood barefoot in the garden and grinned like a witch.

My curtains spat ash at her feet.

THE WALKER

Anna Walsh

The new hotel was one of those places the older guys liked to disparage as a fast business, which I took to mean it served cocktails. Its opening had caused a genuine, and specific distress in the square, igniting panic in the self-satisfied business owners. Mass renovations had begun along the street I lived in, old takeaways and minor laundering businesses closing their shutters and re-opening, bland and clean as a snapping row of newly-polished teeth.

That particular night, I was bored of town, bored of hanging around avoiding people, and walked home the longer way, so I could take a look in. There was nobody on the door, either to welcome me or to tell me to fuck off. The latter was usually the case: my haircut, boots, and sly looks failed to endear me to most publicans. I walked in, trying to figure out if it was one of those perennially half-open places that let you come inside but refuse any service. The golden bar was unmanned, the red ceiling studded with old-fashioned, dim lights. I tested the waters, following the lights, placing one foot onto the thick red carpet of the reception area. I walked along the foyer, and sat down on one of the terrible, crouched leather chairs, my knees knocking off the low table in front of me. The tables were cheap wood, shined to look expensive. I ran my fingers underneath the table, feeling for the rough plywood, tiny splinters attaching to my fingers like velcro. I felt cartoonishly large and undignified, sitting alone with my legs hunched up, unnerved by the landscape of glowing red walls and tiny furniture.

I had called in for a number of reasons. I was curious about the building while it was under construction. It had previously been a run-down arts centre, filled with unframed paintings, wrecked paperbacks, and lino floors. I used to call in semi-regularly to sit around and pretend to read. I loved quietly observing everyone, ascribing a note of sadness to every minor movement. It made me feel like Jean Rhys, with less crying. The staff in the arts centre had been reduced in the past few years; its founding coven of greying middle-aged artists whittled down to a few grad school volunteers living close by, trying to fill their days in ways resembling a job. The grad students wore loose pants and orange socks, black Doc Martens and sported either asymmetrical haircuts or shaved heads. They were all very nice, and I relished feeling sorry for them, relished knowing their almost certain trajectories. It gave me a lonely little kick, to sit and watch things unfold with an almost perverse inefficiency. They organised poetry readings and life-drawing classes, and regularly exhibited 'Women's Art', selling small squares of coastlines and vaginal flowers for two hundred quid.

Generally the back rooms were empty or used for other things. The common area had been a kind of meeting place for locals; older people who found it difficult to maintain friendships or couldn't afford to go out, and English and Philosophy students, younger versions of the curators of the space. The younger students had longer hair, wore single earrings and loudly ingratiated themselves under the guise of making themselves comfortable, taking pride in trying to blend in. They brought cheap cans and tobacco, and bitched at one another in flattened chairs. They watched everything, looking on as I lost a game of chess to one of the older women, her hair fluorescent blue under the buzzing white lights, tipping her cigarette ash precisely into an empty can. I came in with Rose sometimes, who hated the whole scene with its mismatched, shabby decor, and particularly hated the idea of bringing our own cups to drink from. Once, during a discussion about the benefits of private education, a younger student had called her a snob, and she had eagerly agreed, embarrassing me.

* * *

The colour palette of the new hotel was dully chaotic. Aside from the hellish reds of the reception, the walls and floors were drab, dark shades of olive green and sandy yellows. Parched, chalky pinks, yellows and mint were flicked across a dull, sewage green in the hallways. It looked like dandruff in parts. I was used to the generic, lifeless hotel decor in town, neat rectangles of grey canvas art mounted on a cream wall, over a small, pinched single bed. I enjoy the tiny cups of instant coffee, the engineered quiet, the space to lie around. I always feel like I'm packaging myself up in a cardboard box to be posted abroad, somewhere that takes several weeks to get to.

I rubbed my finger along the small ledge, pressing dust between my index and thumb. The cheap white wainscoting along the walls was softening already. The lighting was dim, and made everything look dull, the small, petrified icons of the bathroom signs glowing in the distance. Bad oil paintings of pastoral scenes, of arrogant English men proud of their cows, hung on the walls. The carpet was spongy and my footsteps left faint impressions behind me.

The bathroom was surprisingly spotless, shining and well-lit. I took my time, washing my hands and running them through my hair, slicking short, dark tufts behind my ears. My face was pale, my eyes darkly ringed. It suited me. I wished I was wearing an earring, or a thin necklace. My white shirt was spotted with light stains, and my long, dark green coat depressed me. I splashed water on my face and for a moment I forgot what time it was, what day or whose life it was. I desperately wanted a distraction. I ran my hand up under my shirt, pressing it against my ribs and stomach. I couldn't tell if I was hungry or nauseous.

Rose did not want me to stay with her. It made more sense to turn off my phone, to stop thinking about it, and resume my night-walking activities. Rose did not know the extent of my habits, and I had to practice quite carefully now. She had friends everywhere, and so, naturally, I felt I had plenty of rivals who would like to uncover my secret movements. Rose disliked when I became unavailable to her, particularly because she knew I became self-destructive if left unchecked for too long, and she resented worrying about other people. I walked back to the foyer, enjoying her imagined distress. I felt very sad, and did not know really how to square up to it. My hands were deep in my pockets when I walked straight into someone, the combustive force a relief from my thoughts. I said *excuse me* without looking up, and walked on.

'Excuse me?'

I looked back. A short, middle-aged man, dressed in a wrinkled white shirt and filmy grey trousers, looked perturbed. He rubbed his chin.

'Excuse me.'

'Are you alright pal? You walked right into me!'

He sounded distressed, but I couldn't figure out if it was connected to his swaying, or whether he possessed an amount of decency. I vaguely thought about what I would do if he tried to hit me. I shrugged and kept walking.

'Hey man! You can talk to someone! It can't be that bad!'

Down in the foyer, there was a small congregation near the bar. There seemed to be no staff still, and I doubted any of those present worked there. Not because of the noise and precarious wine glasses, but because they looked well-off and middle-aged. I felt like I was witnessing a badly organised swingers' party.

I wanted a hot drink or a dark liquor, but did not want to place myself in any firing line of drunk, ostensibly straight people. I sat near a window, the sky navy, plumes of cloud spotting across stars. It would have felt romantic if I had not been so numb with heartbreak, the night sky great, and my mind jealously full of people I didn't know, people in love. I thought of Achilles and Patroclus, hating myself for thinking in such overblown narratives, but I was hurting the only way I knew how to, and so I kept dramatising to myself. I didn't know what I longed for – the thoughts of seeing Rose filled me with a misshapen rage, the thought of seeing anyone else engulfed me in tragic boredom and distress. I wanted a cup of coffee with cream, and brown sugar, and a smuggled nip of whiskey. I wanted something badly, something, a sensation or a taste. Night-walking had lost some of its function – I could not stop thinking of her. Maybe I was getting older, a bit ridiculous. I rolled a cigarette.

The group at the bar were shrieking, the men throaty and red, women loosening their grips on one another to become finally selfish, and talk about their dead school friends and sex. I stepped outside to smoke. The night was motionless and cold, darkness distilled. The streets were mostly empty, some stragglers weaving home, streetlights spooling around greedy smiles and lost punchlines.

I didn't want to go back inside. I didn't really want to be or go anywhere, I wanted to throw myself into a crevasse, on a different continent – a hotter, midge-filled one where suicides went unnoticed and were chalked up to things *just being like that* sometimes. There were too few avenues for disappearing here. The crowd inside screamed and laughed. I was surprised I could hear them so clearly from outside. A taxi slowed down along the street, rolling down the window to ask if there was anyone inside. I shrugged. I had recently started ignoring people. It was a small thrill, denying people what they wanted of me and feeling like an asshole.

'Scuse me love, can I rob a smoke off ya?'

I turned. One of the women from the group emerged from the hotel. She had dyed black hair, expensively curled and arranged, visibly split ends sprouting across her shoulders. I didn't want to give her anything.

'Do you have any?'

Her words rolled, unhurried, around in her mouth. I gripped the box of tobacco in my pocket and remained silent. She was slurring a little. Her eyes slid in and out of focus, roving one minute, half-closed the next.

'Actually yeah I do, but it's just rollies.'

There was a pause. She continued looking around me, limply holding a hand out.

'I can make you one though.'

'Oh brilliant, thanks a million. I'm fucking dying for one and I can't buy any in there.'

'Why not?'

'Told my husband I'd quit if he got a vasectomy a few years ago. He still thinks I'm off them.'

I stifled a laugh, a little shocked, unsure of how much fun I could poke at her spouse. She looked drowsy as I rolled, smiling girlishly as I held my lighter out to her. She did not look like a smoker, her skin youthful and teeth white. She took a deep drag, sighing, and looked me in the eye.

'Oh go on yeah, laugh, everyone does. Even his mother knows. I don't care, he's my second.'

'Jesus. Does he not suspect?'

'Ah, he must. But I'd imagine that catching me in the act would only give him the license to take off.'

'Are you not worried he'll see you now?'

She shifted slightly, moving her well-dressed weight from one leg to the other.

'I suppose I should say that I am, shouldn't I. Anyways, go on, thanks for this. You're a star.'

She sucked down on the filter before flicking it out onto the road. She smiled at me serenely and turned inside, almost missing the step into the foyer. She lifted her arm in welcome, her back to me.

'You should come in, have a drink with us. Don't be out here looking miserable.'

Her words receded into the light of the bar. I felt stupid and unwanted, but I kind of wanted to go in and have a drink with them. I wanted to see if her husband would cop the smoking, and if they were swapping partners. I had encountered women like her before and had been both intimidated and well-paid by them. I stood in the doorway, feeling impotent, looking over at the velour, brown cushions on the couches, watching the jerky movements of collective drunkenness. I could not stop feeling sorry for myself, drowned in bad design and wanted only mildly, in the most domestic sense, by someone quite drunk. I wished I could let myself go, wished I could make a move, inconsequential or not, without excoriating myself.

I felt in my coat pocket for my phone, daring myself to turn it on. I looked at it, afraid. My thumb was bleeding. I felt stupid. I could be at someone's house taking bad drugs with someone attractive and boring! I could be eating a bowl of cereal on cold tiles, in baggy pajamas! I could be asleep! I could be doing so many things, and instead I insisted on hurting myself, insisted on skinning the ugly purple hangnails from my thumbs, on keeping myself locked away, rolled up tight as a drum. I wished I could give myself room to slip up and act ridiculous.

* * *

My chest hurt a little as I remembered the last time Rose and I had had a ridiculous night together, in an awful wine bar her uncle owned along the canal. We drank red wine and I fucked her in the bathroom. She bit me on the shoulder, drawing blood. She had pulled back, tittering in delight. A spot of red spread on my white collar, and I checked my injury in the mirror. I had looked good, my neck long and bruised, her head on my shoulder, pouting at our reflection, blending blood and lipstick. She pulled the collar of my shirt up, fumbling buttons open, placing her long gold necklace around my neck.

'Oh my god. My vampire boy.'

I had laughed, pulling her close to me, running my finger along her neck, tapping her in the concave spot where neck meets shoulder.

'My turn.'

'No! Don't! I'll hate it!'

I licked her neck, felt the long, main artery pulsing with wine and adrenaline. Rose always had funny reactions to different alcohols, and red wine made her incredibly horny and jumpy, like a cat in heat. Her skin was hot, the soft dark hairs along her jaw breaking my heart.

'Rose, you might like it…'

She twisted, clamping her hand on my mouth firmly.

'Stop it! I told you! God!'

She pulled herself from my embrace, fixing the neckline of her dress, checking her earrings were still in place. She tossed her hair back and wiped primly at the blood on her lips. She went to leave, and called back at me to hurry. I didn't answer and she turned around to face me.

'Are you okay? Allison? You've gone very pale.'

She walked back over to me, pressing her hand to my forehead.

'Oh no, did I hurt you for real? I'm sorry– I'll get a plaster or something –'

I forced myself to speak. I assured her that she had not hurt me, that I just felt really drunk all of a sudden.

'All of a sudden! You've been hammered since eight!'

She pulled me out the door, waving to her uncle, thanking him for our presumably free drinks. She held my hand outside the small bar, laughing at the wooden sandwich board advertising smudged names of wines. We walked along the canal, stumbling into one another and laughing, fiddling with each other's hair and coats. The long reeds reached out to us from the banks, the marshy ground stippled by small patches of nettles and dock leaves. I felt happy, so happy that I could need nothing more than this, being domesticated with her, knowing what made her laugh. As we walked, something lay darkly in my breast, a gleaming shard of red, of more desire than I knew what to do with it. A jump of saliva on my tongue.

* * *

My mouth filled with saliva as I stood in the foyer, watching the group sing and slur. I felt like I was rushing into myself, suddenly – felt the need to fuck and eat and drink all at once, to do it and walk away afterwards, to eschew worry and consideration and give in. I wanted to put my mouth on warm skin, to tell it what to do. I fiddled with my cuff, pulling at the sleeve of my coat. It would not be difficult, I could slip in and out in an hour. I fell in love with the idea quickly, letting my heart affix itself to the connection I might be able to garner. The woman with black hair was leaning on the bar, rubbing the back of another woman. From where I was standing it looked coaxing, but in reality it was probably less sinister than that, and closer to comforting. I imagined telling her to slap me in the face, her nails leaving a mark, the taste of blood filling my mouth. Putting my hand on her neck, the slip and slide of her giving up to me. I walked around the idea, trying to imagine what would happen if her husband walked in, wondering if I would care if he saw. I knew that I wouldn't: husbands never upset me, and they frequently minded a lot less than one would think.

I sat across from the group, in one of the horrible small chairs. I would sit, and think, and watch them. If something came to pass by my being there, so be it. I would not seek it, and even as I told myself that, I felt myself catching the eye of the woman. Her gaze rested on me for a moment, she was probably trying to figure out why she recognised me. The woman she was beside lifted her head, wiping at her eyes under her glasses. Blonde curls spilled out from her clipped-up hair, and I could see her lipstick was a little smeared. They were both quite handsome, wearing little jewellery, and clinging dresses. I longed for them to ask me how I was, to place a hand on mine. I wanted to walk over to them.

'Hey! Hey! You came!'

The woman was waving and beckoning at me, continuing to rub her friend's back. She looked determined and almost annoyed that I was not responding.

'Hello! Yes I see you, come on!'

She stood up straight, and pulled over a tall stool. She stood until I stood, sighing exaggeratedly, until I made my way across the room. She pushed me onto the stool, parking me in between her and her friend.

'Isn't this lovely! What will you have – eh – sorry, what's your name again?'

I cleared my throat. It felt like I hadn't spoken in hours.

'Allison.'

'Allison! Yeah. Brilliant, you sit there and I'll get you a drink. Red wine or white? Brandy?'

'Eh, red please. Thanks.'

'Great! I'll be back soon, don't move.'

She turned to walk behind the bar, and caught me by my elbow.

'Sorry love, I need a break. I love her, but Christ. Talk to her for a minute will you.'

I turned, annoyed. The blonde woman was staring at her wine glass, sniffling a little. Her nails were painted a pale pink, matching her dress.

'It happens to everyone, and you know, I used to listen to eejits like me saying that and think, nope, no it doesn't, it only happens to pathetic, *boring idiots* who can't keep a man interested for five fucking minutes. Nope, not me, I could do it all, I did everything fucking upside down and backwards for him, I let him use me for whatever he wanted… Are you married? God, listen to me. I'm literally a cliché, crying into horrible white wine… Are you?'

'Am I married?'

She nodded, half smiling.

'No. I almost was.'

'You're better off. It's useless, outdated, bullshit, and love is even worse. Don't even fucking bother. They just fucking – ugh. I'm tired. I'm so bored of being sad over it, you know. I could be doing so much and instead I'm fucking sitting here drunk again and pretty much by myself. No offence.'

'None taken.'

'But you know what the best part of it was. The best part of it was that I still had so much for a while, he still wanted to see me and the kids, still wanted to be friendly with me... '

'Mmm-hmm.'

'And I wasn't able for it! I had to fuck it, really fuck it, so I could cope. You know?'

'Not really.'

'Ugh, you wouldn't. You're so young. You probably have parents that are my age.'

'Not exactly.'

'Well, thereabouts. Well, I just don't know. I feel cracked, really just fucking too cracked up and fucked up. I can't let it go.'

Her eyes were wide, and bloodshot now, her hands in front of her face, making arrow-like movements towards the bar. She looked like she was making some of it up on the spot. It didn't really make a difference, whatever had or hadn't happened had still done this to her.

'I'm not sure what to do now you know. My daughter is so angry with him… Keeps telling me to go on a trip, but I can't really afford it you know… She lives in her own little head. She owns a lot of plants.'

'She sounds cute.'

'She is. Do you know her?'

I shook my head.

'Maybe you'd like her. I'll show you a picture.'

She took out a cracked iphone from her handbag, struggling with her passcode. She swiped through photos, and showed me a woman in her early twenties, with brown, curly hair, glasses, dressed in a yellow coat like Paddington Bear.

'She's very kooky. She wants me to go to a writing class with her, she thinks it would do me good... I don't know. Can you talk to her for me? Tell her to leave me to wallow?'

'I'm not sure I can. You might have to do that.'

'I don't want to! I don't want to! I want everyone to leave me alone!'

I smiled, nodding. 'Yeah.'

'Like you, you're a fine young thing, annoying nobody, smiling away. You're lovely.'

'Haha, I'm not sure many people would agree with you.'

'Fuck them. Fuck them all, girl. Fuck him.'

I flushed.

'You are. Fuck this. You'd be fed up.'

'You really would!'

The woman with black hair offered me a large glass, slopping with wine. She smiled at me, and tipped her head towards her friend, widening her eyes and making an 'o' with her mouth. She sat beside the woman, sipping from her refilled glass.

'John was saying there that he doesn't know what way the thing will go on Monday. He said it depends on Gillian and her father.'

'Oh really.'

'Yeah. We should probably do something '

'I really don't want to, Ger.'

'Well it could be good to do something.'

The blonde woman pressed her hand on my arm, and leaned towards me, whispering.

'This is what I mean. I can't stick this.'

I nodded, not bothering to appear interested anymore. I wanted to leave. I felt flatly bored and couldn't see any good coming from sitting there until six in the morning. There was nothing happening, and the other people in the group were faltering too, slumping close to one another on the chairs, nothing left to confide. I hated this part of a night, being one of a few left standing, feeling exposed as a lush and a partier, someone who wants a thing to continue past its natural end, someone who tries to subvert the inevitable. The funny thing was, anybody who saw me at nights like these would never consider me a partier, or even someone who enjoys themselves. Some of Rose's friends had dubbed me 'Killer' after a birthday dinner and, when I had overheard, the little group had simply shrugged and said, you just always kill the mood. *It's not like I'm not trying,* I said to Rose after. I try with them but they're such cunts sometimes. She had replied, curling into sleep, tucked under the blanket, *that's the thing with them babe, they don't respect anyone who has to try. You're better off not bothering.*

THE CURSE

Heather Parry

What follows is a collated group of abstracts from research papers published over a period of seven years, all authored by one researcher and overseen by her mentor. Though the first papers were published in prominent medical journals, the latter reports could only be found on increasingly obscure websites. Due to the sporadic nature of the publications in which these papers appeared, and the seeming disparity of the subjects, the now-evident link between them was unfortunately not made in time. These abstracts are presented in support of Ms Ahlqvist's proposed release from the facility in which she is currently resident, as the co-authors of this letter consider her voice a necessary one in the fight against the female menace putting the very fabric of our society at risk.

We present these abstracts only for brevity's sake; the full papers can be found at the links below.

1. The Visibility of Menses and the Infertility Epidemic

Diana Ahlqvist and Morton Richt (Mentor)

This paper assesses the spread of the so-called Infertility Epidemic in certain parts of Africa and Asia, in which rates of live births have dropped significantly over a period of twelve months, in predominantly low-income areas. In order to investigate this, we collected water samples from affected areas and tested women seemingly affected by this infertility spread. Though the initial hypothesis of this paper was that a crucial lack of potable water created an unsuitable environment for the washing of reusable sanitary cloths, contributing to an enormous increase in bacterial vaginosis and the spread of papillomaviruses, over the course of the research period a significant number of women urged us to take record of an old wives' tale regarding a link between menstrual blood being seen by another person and the menstruator being latterly rendered unable to conceive. As we explain in the second half of this paper, to our surprise this endured as the most convincing explanation for the epidemic, as there proved to be zero connection between papillomaviruses and the infertile women. In addition, it is notable that the affected women did not experience a cessation of their menses.

2. Understanding Atypical Alexithyma Syndrome (AAS) and its Statistical Co-occurrence with Emotional Detachment Disorder

Diana Ahlqvist and Morton Richt (Mentor)

The purpose of this study was to identify the psychological conditions that give rise to the recently identified Atypical Alexithyma Syndrome, in which sufferers are unable to identify emotions in themselves or in others, and to gain a greater understanding of the co-occurrence of this syndrome with Emotional Detachment Disorder. What our research revealed, however, was that the vast majority of these cases had been misdiagnosed; in fact, individuals thought to be suffering from these two conditions were unable to *feel* emotion rather than being unable to identify it. Though the research group sought for a representative spread of sufferers for this paper, we were only able to find female-identifying or non-binary individuals, a small percentage of whom also exhibited the infertility discussed in our previous paper, published in [redacted]. Each individual involved in the study recounted what they considered to be the moment that their condition manifested; each one had suffered a traumatic loss of a family member and their grief had been witnessed by men in the local community. To quote a popular refrain among participants, 'They saw our tears, that was the start of it.' Individuals report no negative consequences of their lack of emotions; rather they feel released from what they now see as a repressive attachment to actions beyond their control. In the few individuals also declared infertile, some anti-social behaviour has been noted. The authors of this paper would like to stress that this situation requires further research and supporting funding.

3. The Biology and Social Contexts of Global Taste Impairment Diseases

Diana Ahlqvist and Morton Richt (Mentor)

This self-funded study was intended to prove that the apparent spread of a serious taste-impairment disorder throughout certain portions of Asia and Europe had no statistical link with the conditions described in my previous two research papers. To some end, this was a successful endeavour; we found no necessary physiological link between this most recently-defined disorder with either of the previous two conditions. Yet what we did find was a social link between the two; indeed, the spread of a set of ideas that seem to be influencing the behaviours of many in the region – and, as we later found, in countries which share a border with our main area of study. Rising out of the ongoing social unrest in one particular country, the abovementioned taste-impairment disorder was first established in a large number of female inmates, almost all of whom formed part of the PFAR group most identified for their resistance efforts against the national police who have been accused of gender-based violence in their response to political upheaval and the resulting riots in the country. More specifically, all of the women studied self-reported having spat on their arresting officers. After the fact of their arrest, they all, too, self-reported a loss of any taste sensation whatsoever, leading to a lack of interest in food and drink, though it must be noted that they could still feel hunger and thirst, and did respond to these feelings by eating and drinking. As well as conventional food and drink, the incarcerated individuals have reportedly eaten parts of their bedsheets, hay gathered from the forced-work area of the prison and, in a particularly violent incident, one inmate chewed and swallowed, apparently at leisure, the throat flesh of an officer (who has since been suspended for suspected instances of sexual violence). None of these women are set to stand trial, nor are they eligible for parole or release, so it appears that for now, this disorder is contained. However, it must be stated that further resources are necessary, along with greater access to these women, to ensure that further cases of the disorder are properly documented.

4. A Study of Anhidrosis Across Several Continents with a Particular Focus on the Community Response to the Spread of this Condition

Diana Ahlqvist and Morton Richt (Mentor)

For this study, no less than ten distinct teams of researchers were dispatched for a period of several months, each to a particular country to study a particular group. These groups covered a large spectrum of racial and societal identities; having studied the data exhaustively we can find no pattern, genetic or social, that might explain the places in which the aforementioned condition has been documented. The spread is at once random and yet, to divest from rationality for a moment, somehow connected. A quarter of the female researchers who participated in the study have, during or since the research period, reported symptoms similar to those exhibited by the study subjects. The symptoms are these: in the height of the summer/of the rainy season in their country, affected subjects suddenly and with no warning experience a complete termination of their physical responses to external conditions. That is, they no longer feel temperature, pressure, humidity – they can sense nothing that we have subjected them to, short of physical pain, which they still respond to as normal. Resulting behaviours have been so diverse so as to be almost uncatagorisable, but in some notable instances, women in warmer countries have begun to wear many layers during the winter months, while those who have been mostly been forced to cover themselves due to largely inclement conditions in their home country have taken to wearing fewer and fewer clothes. Thanks to the ingenuity of one researcher, we were able to confirm that this condition manifests even when a woman from an exceptionally cold country is taken for a short visit to a very hot one; with the single case of testing, the individual experienced the onset of the condition within 24 hours of landing in the warmer country, though only when released from the testing facility out into the public. I feel it necessary to confirm reports that I am indeed one of the individuals affected since our experiments were carried out. As a short side note, I wish to express my unending gratitude to Dr Richt for his ongoing mentorship and indeed his patience and forgiveness through this difficult period.

5. Non-Sexual Coprophilia in the Elderly as a Potential Result of Pre-Alzheimer's Dementia

Diana Ahlqvist

In response to reports from anthropologists of a growing trend of elderly women smearing excrement on the outside of their homes in the southern regions of [redacted], with an apparent lack of local mythology or religious system that might explain such behaviour, our research teams tentatively approached these areas in order to find any neurological condition underlying such ritualistic actions. Our first assumption was that this may be related to a form of vascular dementia, in which sufferers experience impairment in cognitive functions which can, in turn, lead to semi-feral behaviour. Yet we quickly found that these women, all of whom were over seventy-five years of age, exhibited no evidence of loss of mental faculties. Indeed, the individuals interviewed and tested were in fine health, and could explain their tasks well: once those in the community had glimpsed their excrement, they would no longer need to subsist on food. Though this theory at once defied logic, during the three months of the research period these women were not seen to eat or drink a single thing, and no trickery could be found on extensive examination of their physical surroundings and their bodies themselves. After the research team left the area, we received reports that the women affected had disappeared, taking with them a large number of the town's younger women, who had also left their homes covered in excrement. We consider these women dangerous, and recommend that law enforcement groups put in place measures to stop the spread of these ideas, although we are confident that these warnings will be ignored, as have our last warnings – and we accept that even now it may be too late.

6. Understanding Ritualistic Hypersexuality in Non-Male Populations and The Resulting Social Shifts

Diana Ahlqvist

It can no longer be denied that something significant is happening in the global consciousness. My team, over six months, studied a most alarming phenomenon: that of the cult-like behaviour of a huge number of women or gender-nonconforming individuals in completely disparate communities in several countries around the world. Here follows, for the purposes of stemming this tide, an outline of how this manifests. All cases follow a similar trajectory: an individual, once they have been in contact with others who have already carried out the process, will retreat to her abode, indeed into her private room, for a period of several days to a week; in a number of cases, this period has lasted up to a month. During this time the individual will largely sleep, foregoing food and drink for the most part and completely rejecting social interaction. Eventually the individual will emerge bearing a small vessel or container containing a colourless fluid. The individual will then go out into the street during a time of heavy footfall and, after several moments of screaming and wild behaviour which will draw a crowd, will then throw the contents of the container onto the face or chest of the nearest male. The individual will then flee or retreat for a period of several weeks, to a location currently unknown, and by the time they return to their community, they will be changed; regardless of previous social or romantic attachments they will have paired with another affected individual or will have formed a small group with several women or gender-nonconforming persons with whom they will exhibit gratuitous sexual behaviour. Several of these women have been arrested following homicidal actions, and my research team had some small opportunity to test these women against their own hypotheses: that they could no longer experience desire for or sexual pleasure from the male form or the male physical body. Though the opportunity for experimentation was limited, it appears that this hypothesis may be accurate. The authors of this paper would like to stress the severe need for action to be taken around this subject. Reports of anti-social behaviour, including but not limited to breakouts of small riots, are widespread, and the release of these subjects from the overarching structures under which they have for so long laboured brings with it the risk – if not the certainty – of revolt.

7. The Uprising

Diana Ahlqvist

This paper was intended to quell the growing panic in many circles regarding the now obvious worldwide catastrophe by providing statistical evidence once and for all severing any links between the syndromes, conditions or disorders I have outlined in my last six published papers. And yet. Whilst attempting to gather credible evidence around what is, in the media, being referred to as the Uprising, we in fact uncovered the final, most shocking instance in what must now be considered a linked series of conditions. In several communities in several countries, we have found women (inclusive) and non-binary individuals impervious, in all manners, to physical pain. Our exploration of these communities was prompted by news reports of individuals willingly participating in displays of public sacrificial self-bloodletting. These displays, in which only a small amount of blood was shed onto pavements and fields, have resulted in a complete and total cessation of pain responses in the affected individuals—all of whom, according to our data, also exhibit at least one of the conditions outlined in my last six papers. Our research in this field, however, is scant; from these exploratory trips we have just barely escaped, such is the anarchy inherent in these communities. My team and I strongly advise against any attempts to gather further information on the conditions outlined in my work, for the safety of the researchers cannot be ensured. To be frank, readers: the time for scientific exploration of these groups is over; all that is left is to join or run.

CONTRIBUTOR BIOGRAPHIES

Julia Armfield is a fiction writer with a Master's in Victorian Art and Literature from Royal Holloway University. Her work has been published in Granta, Lighthouse, Analog Magazine, Neon Magazine and Best British Short Stories 2019. She was commended in the Moth Short Story Prize 2017, longlisted for the Deborah Rogers Prize 2018 and was the winner of The White Review Short Story Prize 2018. In 2019, she was shortlisted for the Sunday Times Young Writer of the Year award. Her debut collection, salt slow, was published by Picador in May 2019, and by Flatiron in the US. She lives and works in London.

Jen Campbell is a bestselling author and award-winning poet. Her latest books include The Beginning of the World in the Middle of the Night and The Girl Aquarium. She lectures on the history of fairy tales and the representation of disfigurement. Find out more at www.jen-campbell.co.uk

Sarvat Hasin was born in London and grew up in Karachi. She studied Politics and International Relations at Royal Holloway and then took a masters in Creative Writing at the University of Oxford. Her first novel, *This Wide Night*, was published by Penguin India and longlisted for the DSC Prize for South Asian Literature. Her second book *You Can't Go Home Again* was published in 2018 and was featured in Vogue India's and the Hindu's end of year lists.

She won the Moth Writer's Retreat Bursary in 2018 and the Mo Siewcharran Prize in 2019. Her essays and poetry have appeared in publications such as *On Anxiety*, *The Mays Anthology*, English PEN, and Harper's Bazaar. Her day job is at the Almeida Theatre. Her new novel *The Giant Dark* is forthcoming from Dialogue Books in July 2021.

Beverley Ho is a recent graduate from the University of Edinburgh. Born and raised in the UK, with parents from Hong Kong, she has grown up straddling two cultures. This is reflected in her writing, which aims to lay bare the raw complexities of human relationships. *To Peel an Orange* is her first publication.

Emma Hutton is an Irish writer based in London. Her stories have appeared in *The Mechanics' Institute Review*, *Southword*, *Litro* and *Best Microfiction 2020*. She won the Retreat West Short Story Prize 2019, Mairtín Crawford Short Story Award 2019 and the TSS Flash Fiction Competition 2019.

Susan James is a digital content writer and short story author from Worcestershire. She smashes her computer keys under the influence of too much coffee and with a little black cat on her lap. You'll find her stories dotted across the internet, but she's also been published in *Mslexia* and *The Berlin Reader*. After writing, her biggest passion is travelling. She's been fortunate enough to trek through the Himalayas to Everest Base Camp and made it to the top of Kilimanjaro. She's also been to North Korea. She's a relatively peaceful old soul but does have a degree in War Studies.

Kirsty Logan's latest book is *Things We Say in the Dark*; she is the author of three short story collections, two novels, a flash fiction chapbook, a short memoir, and collaborative work including 'Lord Fox', a live show of spoken word, song and harp music, and 'The Knife-Thrower's Wife', an Angela Carter-inspired album. Her books have won the Lambda Literary Award, Polari Prize, Saboteur Award, Scott Prize and Gavin Wallace Fellowship. Her work has been optioned for TV, adapted for stage, recorded for radio and podcasts, exhibited in galleries and distributed from a vintage Wurlitzer cigarette machine.

Lena Mohamed is a London-based writer who explores race, religion and generational trauma in her work. She has written non-fiction on art, borders and surveillance, and this is her first published work of fiction. Lena holds a BA from UCL and a MA from the Royal College of Art.

Heather Parry is a Glasgow-based writer and editor. She won the 2016 Bridge Award for an Emerging Writer, the Cove Park Emerging Writer Residency in 2017 and was a prizewinner in the 2019 Mslexia Short Story Competition. Heather's work explores self-deception, transformation and identity. She is the co-founder and editor of Extra Teeth magazine.

Leone Ross is Jamaican/British fiction writer and editor. She is a three-time novelist and her short stories have been translated into Spanish, French and Slovak. Her first novel was nominated for the Orange Prize for Literature. The Washington Post described her second novel as "delicious...". Her first short story collection,

Come Let Us Sing Anyway published in 2017 was widely acclaimed: the Times Literary Supplement called her 'a master of detail'. The Guardian called the collection 'remarkable...searingly empathetic, outrageously funny...". Leone judges international writing competitions. Her next novel, a love story about a chef addicted to hallucinogenic moths, is out in April 2021 with Faber & Faber and FSG.

Stephanie Victoire was born in London to a French-Creole Mauritian family. She is an author of short works published in various anthologies and her own collection, *The Other World, It Whispers*, published by Salt Publishing, which was longlisted for the 2017 Edge Hill Prize. She has written both fiction and non-fiction short works for BBC Radio, and articles about her spiritual and holistic knowledge and experiences, published at The Numinous, Oh Comely Magazine and The Cherry Revolution. Although back in the UK for now, Stephanie has travelled to over thirty countries across five continents. She continues to pursue a life of profound experiences, ancient and indigenous wisdom, culture and connection through travel and volunteer work. She is currently writing a non-fiction personal development and wellbeing book as well as other works of fiction.

Anna Walsh is an Irish writer based in Glasgow. They have had poetry and prose published in *Fallow Media*, *Spamzine*, and the *Stinging Fly*, among others. They have work forthcoming in the *So Hormonal* anthology with Monstrous Regiment Publishing. They are currently working on a short story collection, and their debut poetry collection will be published in 2020, in conjunction with the Small Trans Library.

Eley Williams lectures at Royal Holloway, University of London.

Lara Williams is a writer based in Manchester. Her novel *Supper Club* was published in Spring 2019 by Hamish Hamilton (UK) and Putnam & Sons (US). It won The Guardian's Not The Booker prize. Her short story collection Treats was published by Freight Books in 2016 and in the US by Flatiron in 2017 under the title A Selfie As Big As The Ritz. The collection was shortlisted for the Republic of Consciousness Prize and longlisted for the Edge Hill Prize.

Anna Wood's first book of short stories, Yes Yes More More, will be published next year by The Indigo Press. She writes about music (mainly) for Mojo, The Quietus and Caught By The River, and she's also an editor and a copywriter. Anna has an MA in creative writing from UEA and has been a fellow at the Fine Arts Work Center in Provincetown and at the Elizabeth Kostova Foundation in Sozopol. She is planning a beguinage.

RESOURCES

The resources listed here are just a starting point. All are based in the UK but there are many international organisations out there to help around bereavement, abuse, mental health and LGBTQ+ issues.

Mental Health, Trauma and Bereavement

Samaritans To talk about anything that is affecting your mental health, you can contact Samaritans 24 hours a day, 365 days a year. You can call 116 123, email jo@samaritans.org. The Welsh Language Line is 0300 123 3011, 7-11 PM every day.

Black Minds Matter connects Black people to therapists. They have recently raised funds to provide reduced cost or free therapy for clients. https://www.blackmindsmatteruk.com/services.

CALM UK. If you identify as male, you can call the Campaign Against Living Miserably on 0800 58 58 58 between 5 PM and midnight every day. They also have a webchat service.

Respond supports people with learning disabilities, autism or both who have experienced trauma in their lives. 020 7383 0700

LGBTQ+

Gendered Intelligence runs a range of youth groups in London, Leeds and Bristol for young trans people, non-binary and questioning young people aged under 21*. They also run a peer-led support group in London for those aged 18-30. You can contact them for support http://genderedintelligence.co.uk/contact/email

Stonewall Housing This national charity ensures LGBT people can live in safer homes free from fear. Their free, confidential advice line and self-referral systems are still running. They also have simple guidelines for self-isolating. 020 7359 5767

Gender Trust National Helpline For information on Trans* issues 01527 894838

LAWA LBTQ+ (Latin American Women's Aid) LBTQ service in Spanish, Portuguese and English offers information, advocacy and support in a wide range of areas. These include domestic violence and other gendered forms of violence, welfare benefits, housing and emergency accommodation, LBTQ specific services, talking therapy, career and employment advice, skills development and community integration. 0207 275 0321

Opening Doors London (ODL) is a charity that supports LGBT+ people over the age of 50. They provide a befriending service in London. and a telefriending service for those who are based outside of London. Call 020 7239 0400 https://www.openingdoorslondon.org.uk

LGBT Foundation A Manchester based charity offering mental health services and resources to the gay community. This includes befriending, free counseling and a support helpline. 0345 3 30 30 30 http://www.lgbt.foundation/

Birmingham LGBT Centre Voluntary organisation providing advice and support to LGBT+ people in Birmingham. Offers counselling, well-being services and a wide range of support groups. 0121 643 0821 http://www.blgbt.org/

LGBT Helpline Scotland A telephone helpline for LGBT+ people living in Scotland. The helpline can be accessed by phone on 0300 123 2523 during the following hours: Tuesdays from 12-9pm, Wednesdays from 12-9pm, Thursdays from 1-6pm, Sundays from 1-6pm. https://www.lgbthealth.org.uk/services-support/helpline/

LGBT Youth is a Scotland-based charity for LGBTI young people, working with 13-25 year olds across the country. It runs youth groups around the country and also has a text helpline you can contact on weekdays on 07984 356 512. https://lgbtyouth.org.uk/groups-and-support/

Cara Friend is an LGBT+ organisation offering services across Northern Ireland. The helpline is open Monday-Friday from 1pm-4pm, with additional evening cover on Wednesdays from 6pm-9pm and can be accessed by phone on 0808 8000 390 or via email at switchboard@cara-friend.org.uk https://cara-friend.org.uk

Drug and Alcohol Abuse

Antidote is a service that offers information and support exclusively to LGBT+ people around drugs, alcohol and addiction. Part of London Friend's service. If you have a query relating to drugs and alcohol you can call the Antidote team during office hours on 020 7833 1674

Domestic Abuse/ Sexual Assault

FLOW Finding Legal Options for Women Survivors. They work with LGBT+ survivors of Domestic Violence Abuse and offer support. 0203 745 7707 or email flows@rcjadvice.org.uk

Women & Girls Network A free service that supports women in London who have experienced violence, or are at risk of violence. 0808 801 0660 or advice@wgn.org.uk

Ashiana addresses violence against women in BME communities across the UK 0208 539 0427 https://www.ashiana.org.uk/

Survivors UK (male, boy, trans+ survivors of rape) rape phone 02035983898 or email isva@survivorsuk.org. https://www.survivorsuk.org

Angelou Centre A specialist helpline for agencies who are working with Black and minority survivors of domestic and sexual violence who have no recourse to public funds. referrals@angelou-centre.org.uk

Muslim Women's Network provides support and advice for women who may face additional obstacles because of religion or culture in getting help in situations of forced marriage, domestic or sexual abuse. www.mwnuk.co.uk 0800 999 5786 (Mon-Fri 10am – 4pm) / text 07415 206936 info@mwnhelpline.co.uk

Jewish Women's Aid is a specialist organisation in the UK supporting Jewish women and children affected by domestic abuse & sexual violence. https://www.jwa.org.uk/ DVA helpline: 0808 801 0500 Sexual Violence helpline: 0808 801 0656